Valerian

PRIDEFUL MAGICK COLLECTION
BOOK THREE

TENTH ANNIVERSARY EDITION

HOLLOW RYAN

Valerian

Second Edition

Published by Hollow Ryan

Ebook ISBN: 978-1-968729-07-3
Trade Paperback ISBN: 978-1-968729-06-6
Hardcover ISBN: 978-1-968729-08-0

Cover elements courtesy of:
Vintage Damask by DarkMoon_Art via Pixabay.com
Realistic Smoke Fog by Hakan Kaçar via Vecteezy.com
Valerian Flowers Herb Real by fietzfotos via Pixabay.com

Cover Design by Christiana Nehmsmann
Interior Design by Christiana Nehmsmann

Books By Hollow Ryan

Prideful Magick Collection

Ivy

Oleander

Valerian

Hawthorn

Avens

Demon Kin

Demon Kin: The Queen

Demon Kin: The Lovers

TABLE OF CONTENTS

1. Scars	1
2. Memories	6
3. Drug of Choice	16
4. Do What Ye Will	25
5. Damaged	33
6. Séance	45
7. On the Fly	54
8. Crown Jewel	66
9. Threat	77
10. Legacy	88
11. Battle	97
12. Respect	108
13. Heartsick	118
14. Compare	129
15. Monotony Kills	140
16. Shoebox	147
17. Pity	157
18. Soulmates	165
19. Futile	176
20. Dealing	184
21. Coming Clean	196
22. Hero	205
23. Lighthouse	217
24. Ashes on the Wind	227
25. Still	238

26. Drowning 248

27. Fickle 256

28. Free 263

29. Peace 270

This one is for me.
We all have our dark times.
We have to depend on ourselves to find the light.

Chapter One

SCARS

One day, I would pay the balance for the damage done. When I was done inflicting it.

Every scar marked a day that I would atone for. Four hundred and twenty-seven had come to pass.

It wasn't that I wanted to hurt myself. I needed to. More than the compulsion and routine, I burned so that I would *feel* something again. Anything.

Midnight struck and I took a deep breath while I held my left arm out in front of me. Staring at a spot just above my elbow, I released the magick in a familiar spell that brought to me the delicious pain that I deserved. Pain that I had earned. Soon, the skin transformed into an angry red as the heat seared it from within.

As the design began to form, the burning started to feel more like acid, causing me to clench my teeth against a scream. My right hand curled into a fist and I began to pound on my thigh. At the same time, my left arm tensed, the agony shooting along the nerves all the way up into my shoulder. It coalesced in the star-shaped scar over my left breast before bursting forth and blazing down my arm once more in the last brutal second of completion.

At last, I was able to throw my head back and take in ragged gasps of air while the heat began to subside. Pain still pulsed in the skin, but it was fading into a throbbing ache rather than searing torment. With the same pace, the redness began to fade, leaving a raised white scar where the skin had been smooth a moment ago.

When my heart rate fell into a more natural rhythm, I lowered my head to stare at the new addition. The oak leaf was fitted in amongst the hundreds of ivy leaves that coated my upper arm. One other oak leaf rested near the top of my shoulder, marking the anniversary of my first trip down Old Grove Road. In two more days, I would add my second apple blossom for the day that I met my beloved mentor, Morgan LeFayette.

My eyes closed as the memories attempted to resurface. It wasn't hard, now, to push them back. Not like it was at first. On certain days, however, I let them come.

Somewhere behind that black wall in my mind, I found myself back on the old dirt road. Oak trees stood as sentinels, lining either side of the road at equal spaces. Between them, the young trees and ferns grew up with a surprising rapidity. A playful breeze tossed the leaves, sending up the scent of mint from the scrubby plants that lined part of the road. It was a fantasy of mine that promised tranquility.

One that was ripped away the moment I pictured my two best friends standing in the middle of Old Grove Road. Nathan Richards and Matthew Graham. One who I revealed was my mentor's grandson, and the other who'd been my first boyfriend. Nathan and I had sat side by side on a school bus and in class for four years without really talking. Still, we knew we were there for each other. And Matt had been the first person in Cedar Creek to be interested in me in a personal manner. It was part of my greatest heartbreak, having to leave them both behind. Of all the people to know what I was capable of, Nathan was the most aware of my abilities.

As I thought about him, the first of my scars began to warm and I rubbed at it through my shirt. Unlike the other ivy leaves, the most important ones spread from my left breast, across my collarbone, and merged into the pattern of my left arm. The first was created beside the star-shaped scar left by a lightning strike on the day of my Ascension, right before Morgan committed suicide.

Of all the days that could have caused everything in me to snap, I might have thought that would be it. It wasn't. Not until the day I left Cedar Creek did I feel like everything that made me *me* was chipped away. My compassion, forgiveness, honesty, and hope withered away beneath the harsh glare of my reality. Worse than that, a fierce wind came along and tore my pride, honor, and confidence out of my grasp. When I was uprooted, I had but self-loathing and wrath to cling to.

And I had used them.

To most people, the scars in my arm would be the equivalent to cutting. It offered me the control I was lacking in my life. Using my magick to hurt myself seemed like an unfathomable cry for help. And using my magick to hide it helped me to deal with the shame of having done it in the first place.

Yet, my scars were more than that. Each one created at midnight, marking every day that I spent away from my real home. They were my calendar. Sands in an hourglass, keeping track of the passage of time.

Chapter Two

MEMORIES

When one memory was allowed to slip through the cracks, it was inevitable that others should follow. After shoving thoughts of Matt and Nathan back behind the black wall, I couldn't halt the memory of our first move after Cedar Creek.

Once I was cleared of the murder charges surrounding Morgan's suicide, my dad had made it clear that we would not be staying in a town that had plastered me all over the local news for such a heinous crime. Even though I was innocent, it had taken time for the hype to die down, and it had taken even longer for the court of public opinion to acknowledge the wrongs done to me.

Despite that, I had wanted to stay. Though I

was cracked and a little broken after the ordeal, I was every bit the Marine's daughter. I was every bit the Alexandria Ryder that had faced down a whole department of cops at the age of nine and told them nothing about the life and death of Alyssa Mae Rice, the ghost who first introduced me to all the wonders of my magickal potential. In the five years between the discovery of her body and the trial over my mentor's suicide, my Ryder Pride had grown to formidable degrees. To me, it took no thought to believe I would stand my ground and face down any who would dare speak lies about me.

It was a chance denied to me by my father's rash decision. Thus, he applied for a base transfer. By that July, it had been granted and we'd begun packing.

Granted, I didn't go quietly. We fought for weeks before that day. Which added to the reason I had grabbed the tiniest ivy leaf I could from outside my bedroom window, pressed it to my chest, and had my magick trace it into my skin. If I had to leave Cedar Creek, I was damn well taking a piece of it with me.

By the time we arrived in Virginia, I was

fractured enough that wrath was all I harbored. I'd already figured I was a source of embarrassment for my dad, and that was why he took me away from where everyone knew about me. When we reached Virginia, however, I decided to deepen his chagrin over me. I was ready to punish him, and I did.

Our first weekend on base, I bought a box of cheap black hair dye. Taking some kitchen scissors, I chopped my hair and dyed it. Almost before my parents could finish reaming me about it, I went out and got my nose pierced. Though it was just a tiny stud–I'd never favored real nose rings of any kind–my dad's temper went through the roof.

Of course, the last straw was when I developed a penchant for skipping school. Though I wasn't failing, my attendance record had sparked a phone call to my mom that sent her over the edge. I spent most of what time we had left in Virginia in the confines of my bedroom. My dad's next transfer didn't come through until after the end of the school year.

Memories of Hawaii surfaced as I pushed myself up off the toilet. Turning on the cold water in the sink, I let it run over my fingertips as I thought about the day that put everything in a far different perspective. For my parents as well as myself.

For the first time in a long time, my mother smiled when I entered the room. Not because she was glad to see me, but because she was relieved that the circumstances of our move couldn't help but be better than where we last were. Given that there was no school in session for me to skip, everything was bound to be easier. Without acknowledging her, I walked past, camera in hand. The other reason for her to be relieved: I was back to traipsing about outdoors, where I was the most content.

Ever since we arrived on Oahu, I'd taken to exploring as much of the island as possible. Walking, however, I wasn't able to make it off of the base. Of course, while we were still in Virginia, I'd learned how to avoid walking everywhere. When I had first realized I could teleport, there had been a lot going on that allowed me to gloss over it as just another gift from my Ascension. In

Virginia, however, I'd begun to utilize every bit of the magick I held within me.

Which was why I went from standing in my kitchen to flashing halfway across the island to Sacred Falls State Park. Though it had its share of tourists like the rest of the island, it was one of those locations where you weren't expected to interact. With the camera around my neck, I looked just like every other passerby that didn't belong there.

After a while, I wandered away from the waterfalls and started taking the hiking trails that wound through the other parks and reserves. I was maybe twenty minutes away from the falls when I realized that the other hikers had all paused, gathering around some small section just off the path. Keeping away from the crowd, I used my ability of remote viewing to see what they were gawking at.

A grass mat was laid out on the ground with a Native Hawaiian stretched out on it. Beside him sat two other men. One had two instruments in his hand, a metal-tipped one that looked like a hoe, and a rod that he was hitting it with. Black lines were left in the man's skin as the hoe-like instrument injected ink into him. Every few minutes, the rhythmic tapping would cease and the second man would wipe away the excess ink, leaving the design exposed for the next application. For several long minutes, the entire group watched as the man received the traditional tattoo. When it was done, the crowd began to disperse. I couldn't move.

Almost everyone was gone, but I stood across the path, staring at the two men as they began to clean up their instruments and work area. Then the older man, who'd been giving the tattoo, looked up and met my gaze. In an instant, I recognized some of my own talents in him. It was the first time in a long time that I felt I'd found a kindred spirit.

Raising his hand a little, he put a halt to his assistant's work, and instead motioned for the grass mat to be rolled out again. Then he gestured me over to him. I moved without thought, glad to be with someone who understood me, even a little. While he cleaned off his instruments, he gestured with his head for me to lie down. After kneeling on the mat, I pulled my shirt over my head and stretched out on my stomach. Since my hair passed the upper tie of my bikini by less than an inch, I knew that it wouldn't be in the way. Which turned out to be a good thing, since I felt the strange instrument settle right between my shoulder blades, overtop my spine.

For several hours, I was stretched out upon the mat, feeling the pressure of the tapping travel along my nerves. It didn't hurt. Instead, it sent little shocks through my system every few minutes, to remind my body that something was being done to it. After all of the burnings, however, my pain sensors couldn't even consider the punctures as worthy of their time.

Soon enough, I became the thing for people to gawk at, but I didn't care. With as long as it was taking for me, they kept walking after a few minutes. By the time the older man finished, no one was around. From the corner of my eye, I watched the assistant pick up a squirt bottle and a clean paper towel. Water splashed over my back and several minutes were dedicated to cleaning up the smeared ink and blood, with the bottom tie of my bikini acting as a dam for the liquid when it tried to travel down my entire back.

The moment he was done, I sent my magick

out to do some more remote viewing. This time, I was looking down on myself, studying the dark designs that had taken a long time to create and fill in. What I found there looked like a burning compass. Tongues of flame spread out from the center spiral. The longest two points stretched along my spine, looking more like jagged lightning. Yet, the two longest on the sides looked just like a dancing flame. All of it connected back to a spiral that first looked as if it were going one way, but at second glance appeared to be going the other. An optical illusion in the skin. There was no expressing the amount of talent or magick needed to create such a visual wonder.

When I recalled my magick, I closed my eyes and could feel the image sinking into my skin. It was becoming a part of me. Reading me and identifying how it belonged. The magick in it was binding with the magick in me, each one recognizing the other as a part of me. Somehow, it almost felt like the skin between my shoulder blades had been holding the pattern all along, and his job was to make it visible.

After a while, I pushed back up onto my knees and looked at both of the men. They had given me a gift by performing the tattooing. I needed to do something in return. Something only a witch could do. Yet, when I looked again at the man who gave me the tattoo, he shook his head, a smile transforming his wrinkled face. Once I was off the mat, they proceeded to clean up their things before disappearing back along one of the trails.

I waited a few more minutes before throwing my shirt on and teleporting back to my own house. For a while, I just wanted to stand in front of a mirror and stare at the design, and try to figure out why it felt so right to have it in my skin.

I didn't hide my tattoo like I hid my scars. Most of my shirts covered it, but if they didn't, it wasn't something to stress over. Not that my parents saw it that way. Thus my dad applied for yet another transfer. Which was why Oceanside, California was the last favor he was granted. If I screwed this one up, there were no more transfers and my dad's career would pretty much be dead.

Part of me cared.

Most of me didn't.

We made it to Oceanside right before the school year started, and I put the extra time to good use. One of the first things I did was track down a salon. In the time between me getting the tattoo and moving, my hair had grown about three more inches. They vanished at the salon as they transformed my brown hair from something that looked like it'd gotten caught by a lawn mower into a more deliberate style involving layers. I also had them dye it black again. A fact my parents were most displeased about when I got home.

Not that it mattered. It had been made clear long ago that they could no longer control what I did. Which was why I hid the calendar in my arm. If they weren't strong enough to stop me, there was no point in them ever knowing about it.

Chapter Three

DRUG OF CHOICE

Tired of the memories, I escorted them one by one behind that black wall in my mind, slamming the door shut behind them. After shutting off the water, I left the bathroom and crossed the hallway to my room. Even though it wasn't that late, I was still glad that my parents' room was on the other side of the house. Most days, it was best for all of us not to interact too much.

I settled in front of my altar, which rested on a low coffee table on the other side of my dresser. It was adorned with several items related to the Craft, but I needed none of them at the moment. All I wanted was my dose.

Most people didn't realize that valerian was the plant most often used in their sleeping medications, but witches often used a tincture for sleepless nights. For me, every night was a sleepless night. Despite the fact that fatigue clung to me like a second skin, it was impossible for my mind to shut down the way it was supposed to. So, I took a dose of valerian.

It hadn't taken me long to realize that valerian did more for me than put me to sleep. Even though I started off with small doses, I'd hit many of the side effects right away. Of course, it was impossible to tell what was caused by the valerian versus what was caused by my situation. After all, apathy, depression, and night terrors had all begun before my doses. Yet, as I'd had to up the dosage over the past year, I'd begun to feel the drowsiness and dizziness as well. I'd come to terms with the fact that, even if the valerian didn't cause it, it certainly exacerbated things.

Which was fine by me. Draining the vial in one gulp, I made a face and set it back on the altar. Getting to my feet, I stretched as I waited for the drowsiness to really hit me. What I was looking forward to the most, however, was the morning numbness. Right after the trial had ended, I'd learned to generate more than enough on my own; however, that was the greatest blessing of the valerian. The apathy that it increased could get me through almost an entire school day if I worked it right. And with how school was going at this point, I could see myself increasing the doses at least two more times before the year was out.

Most people needed caffeine to get through their day. Others looked to stimulants. For me, valerian was my drug of choice.

The dose was too heavy. I knew that as soon as the dream began, and I lacked all of the urgency that usually accompanied it. Blackness stretched out all around me, as if I were trapped inside of the box in the back of my mind. Yet, in this place, there were no memories to plague me. Instead, there was only one person who reigned here.

Turning in a circle, searching vainly in the dark for nothing, I thought I could hear his voice calling my name. It always started off faint, but grew as he drew closer to me. Even then, I often would break into a sprint, eager to see him one more time. When I had a heavier dose, however,

I remained sluggish even in that aspect.

Not for long, though. As the dream required, I began to walk, and I continued to hear a voice calling for me. With every step, the numbness began to fade. Fast. After a few yards, my head whipped from side to side, searching for the source as Nathan's voice seemed farther away than before.

Picking up the pace, I settled into a steady lope as I yelled his name. The next time, he sounded closer. Again, I picked up the pace to a jog. His name flew from my throat in rapid bursts, so that I couldn't hear if he called back. Then I paused for a moment, standing stiff as a statue, as I waited on his reply. The moment I heard my name, I was off in that direction.

This nightmare was the same as it always was, however, and when he came into sight, my stomach dropped. Even so, my heart began to race and I took off into a sprint. The smile spread across my face, feeling foreign and unnatural even in my dream.

My nightmare.

"Nathan!" I shouted as I raced toward him.

He turned to see me, a familiar, warm smile

spreading across his face. "Lex!" He started racing toward me, both of us on a direct collision course.

Not that we would ever collide. The closer we got to one another, the faster the blackness bore down on us. We could sense it closing in, a thick wall that would slam between us before we could cross the distance. As a result, we pushed ourselves harder. Faster. Saving each of our breaths for the next burst of energy shooting through our bodies, ignoring the pain in our sides and the sweat on our palms.

Nathan and I were desperate to reach each other. Which was why we never would. I reached a few more steps over what I had done last night when the wall slammed into place. Before I could stop myself, an anguished cry erupted from my throat and I dropped to my knees. My heart was broken all over again.

When I woke up, my head was in a thick, heavy fog. It dulled everything around me into a more manageable spectrum. There was even a smile on my lips as I stumbled toward the bathroom, my vision blurring.

After a quick shower, I used my magick to pull the steam from the mirror, glad to note that I got every drop of condensation in one pull. It had been a strange decision to make when we left New England, that I would not hide my magick. That I would do as I pleased, no matter the consequences. Had I not already borne consequences for actions not my own? Was it not time that I was able to live my life as I desired, rather than forcing myself to bend to a weaker will?

It was why I cut my hair and dyed it the first time, after all. I'd suffered long enough to make the choice that all decisions about my life would be mine. If I wanted to cut my hair, I would cut it. Though I'd never before thought of getting a piercing, I didn't regret the stud in my nose. My tattoo was a part of me that I was glad of.

Yet, not one choice that I made could not be undone.

My hair would grow out, leaving its natural color to show once more. If I wanted, I could even allow the hole in my nose to close up. I even possessed the talent to pull the ink from my back, leaving the skin as unblemished as the day I was born.

Not that I would. Like my magick, they were all things that made up who I was. Each one was a lesson and experience that I had more than deserved. If my reward was the small marks upon my body that said I survived those changes, so be it.

After a moment of staring at myself in the mirror, I was careful in the application of my makeup-the kind that my dad detested, but my mother saw no harm in. It was another of those things I had thought I would never bother with, but long minutes spent in front of a mirror focusing on making exacting lines with liquid eyeliner was kind of soothing. When I was done, I looked good in a way I had never thought to see myself. It was rewarding, in its own way.

When I went to get dressed, I almost sighed at the lack of choices I had in wardrobe. It was easier to hide the scars beneath clothes than keeping a glamour in place, so I'd stocked up on several three-quarter-sleeve shirts before school started. Yet, last night showed me that I would soon have to move below the elbow to keep my calendar going. Which meant winter couldn't come fast enough, when long sleeves in California wouldn't be remarked upon too much.

Without bothering to walk, I went from my bedroom to the kitchen in an instant, uncaring whether or not my parents were in attendance. Not that I expected my father to be. He was out the door while I was in the shower most days. We considered it in his best interest, since I had a habit of pissing him off with my apathy and sarcasm before he had to work. My mother, on the other hand, sat at the kitchen table and watched in silence as I poured myself a glass of orange juice and took an apple from the fridge. I didn't stick around to see if she would talk to me today. Ever since Hawaii, there had been nothing for us to say.

I drifted out of my house after breakfast and almost surprised myself by deigning to take the bus to school. Of course, if I got on the bus, it was pretty much the most assured way that I would go to school. Those that saw me were witnesses of the silent commitment I'd chosen to make that day, and so I considered myself honor bound to follow through.

Slinking toward the back of the bus, I found

myself in the last half-seat beside the emergency exit. Across from me sat a girl with platinum blonde hair that had blue tips in a light-to-dark ombré. She usually paired it with a purple beret that she had to take off during school, and there were holes in her bottom lip where her snake-bites would have fit if they were permitted at our school. I appreciated her style, and enjoyed what she did with her hair, but I never said one word to her.

Due in most part to the lanky boy with ink-black hair that hovered over her shoulder. He stood in the very back of the bus, staring down at her with an expression that shifted between remorse and longing. Not that she noticed. No one but me could see him. The reason being the several slashes running from his wrists almost to his elbows on either arm. It was also the reason I pretended not to see him. I'd had someone I love commit suicide. As far as I was concerned, he could suffer with the torment of that mistake. I held no pity for him.

Chapter Four

DO WHAT YE WILL

When we reached the school, I didn't bother to wait in the line of those about to disembark. Instead, I went from my seat to the sidewalk in a blink, not caring who saw. Not that it would have mattered if anyone did. What could they do? Report me to the nearest crusader?

I'd always found that funny about books concerning witches, that there was always some overseeing council or some such that determined how they lived. Like any one of us would accept someone else as an authority over our decisions and choices. Wiccans, at least, lived by the Threefold Law, determining that what was sent out came back times three. It was also something I tended to live by, since I thought it was similar enough to the Golden Rule that it seemed logical. The Wiccan Rede stated: An' it harm none, do what ye will. Which was the same as saying: Do unto others as you'd have done unto you.

Overall, it was a belief that still held strong in myself, but I'd also changed my ideas of what I determined acceptable behavior. I also had a habit of correcting what I considered unacceptable behaviors in those who proved inferior to me. There were more than a few individuals that had learned harassment would not benefit them in any way. That, too, I did not regret.

For several moments, I lingered outside of the school, unwilling to enter until the last possible moment. Slipping out of my tennis shoes, I let my bare feet settle into the grass, attempting to ground myself before the day started.

Since grounding and centering both were methods to keep a body and mind attached to the living energies of the world, it proved most difficult when I was filled with valerian. The apathy caused for a disconnect with everything, which is what allowed for the drowsy dizziness. Even so, I wouldn't have traded a clear head for my foggy one. I'd never survive the day.

The bell sounded in a shrill, insistent tone and I released a sigh. After slipping my feet back into my shoes, I let my body fade through the distance to my first class. As was usual, the desk in the back corner of the room, farthest from the door and with direct sights all around me, was empty. It had taken a few shameless coercions to make sure that no one else was fool enough to sit there, but now it was identified as my seat, even if I didn't show up for class.

My book blinked into existence in my messenger bag as I took my seat. I never carried my things anywhere, and I had yet to even see my locker. Everything I needed resided in my bedroom, so I just took it and returned it from there.

By the time class began, I had relaxed in my chair and closed my eyes. If I wanted to keep the numbness intact, I needed to doze at least a few minutes every class. Becoming too awake or aware could harm my defense mechanism more than anything.

Class had been in session for almost twenty minutes when I heard my teacher inquire, "What is your opinion, Miss Ryder?"

In an instant, my eyes snapped open and

I unleashed my magick on the unsuspecting teacher, searching for the answer in his mind. As he was asking for my opinion, however, the answer wasn't available. The question was.

Derision rose up inside of me, threatening my emotion-blocking dam as I scoffed, "Do I think a person's psychology is affected most during pre-pubescence or adolescence? Childhood, most definitely. What you learn then will settle into you like a foundation stone. Everything else will be built upon that, whether you realize it or not."

Before he had to ask, I had but to think of my Ryder Pride-the nickname my mother gave to the excessive trait bred throughout my father's side of the family-and the magick that had blossomed in me at the age of nine. My confidence and arrogance, even my stubbornness and compassion had all developed before I'd reached double-digits. Yet, it was all of those that carried me through the rest of my life so far.

What happened when I was thirteen affected me, no doubt about it. That didn't mean it had defined me. It made me bitter, hostile, and vengeful, yes. But it was still nothing more than an extension of my pride, stubbornness, and arrogance. The foundations had been in place for over a decade. I'd just built upon them.

For a moment, the teacher seemed more shocked that I had answered than by my answer. Another minute of me glaring at him, however, transformed his expression into one of curiosity. Given that he seemed skilled enough to read faces, he must have decided that seeking the truth wasn't in his best interest when he studied mine, because he turned from me and addressed questions to other students.

Closing my eyes, I tried to tamp down my ire before it made it past the last of my defenses. I didn't want to feel or think or bother with humanity. If I could put an end to this emotion, my valerian might carry me through the rest of the day yet. I'd be happy if it took me as far as lunch.

By the end of class, I knew it wasn't going to survive the first hour. Right before the bell was set to ring, my psychology teacher moved throughout the room, passing out graded papers. Yet, what he set on my desk was a note that said to see him after class. I had to talk myself into staying when the insistent ring of the bell shouted through the school. Though it would have been easy to escape him, I was still hopeful that I could salvage some of my apathy by reacting with open disinterest to whatever it was he said.

"Miss Ryder, could you come up here please?" He didn't look up from the pack of papers that he was examining, and I knew they were mine.

I walked in an odd, normal pace across the room and stood in front of his desk. Saying nothing, I stared at him with a bland expression. The sooner he was done with his spiel, the sooner I was free to go. At the rate my day was going, I wouldn't be heading to my next class, but I would be getting as far from him as was possible.

"Miss Ryder, how long did it take you to complete this assignment?" Again, he didn't look at me as he flipped another page.

"A few minutes," I answered with a shrug.

"Did you have any help on this assignment?"

"Didn't need any." I had all the help I needed from the answer key in his head; I didn't even know what all the questions said.

"Were the concepts covered in this easy enough for you to grasp, then?" His poking and prodding was wasting time that I didn't have.

"I've been to a lot of schools. More than

enough is easy for me to grasp," I remarked, releasing the half-truth without a blink.

The teacher nodded, flipping to the last page and turning it to face me. "I can understand that, but I don't understand why you chose to leave these sections blank."

In truth, I hadn't bothered to read them or try to answer them when I'd filled out the papers that were a majority of multiple-choice questions. So, I told him that. "I didn't want to answer them."

"Why not?" In an instant, his voice had switched to psychologist mode. Too bad for him that my head was impervious to his skillset. The reverse wasn't true.

"I didn't want to. There doesn't need to be another reason."

He didn't get irritated like the other teachers I'd had this conversation with–which meant they had warned him about my attitude–but instead looked at me with that pathetic 'I want to help you' stare that most adults gave when they thought someone wasn't living up to their full potential. It was an expression I deemed pathetic because their idea of someone's potential was based upon their own goals and ambitions. I'd yet to have someone give me that look when they knew my true potential.

"Was it something about these questions?"

"No. There was no other reason. I'd done as much as I was willing to, and chose not to do any more. There was no need."

"Alexandria," he began.

For a moment, I thought about going off on him. Inform him that I knew everything said about me. How I was despondent, disinterested, and lacked respect for my education. Including how I refused to do most of my homework, did not show up for about a quarter of my classes, or responded with unconcern when threatened with disciplinary action. It was the kind of interest in my life that I was specific in not wanting.

The second bell saved me from having to set him straight. I gave him my most disinterested stare and announced, "I'm late." Without another word, I marched out of the room.

Chapter Five

DAMAGED

My second hour class stood between me and the nearest exit, and my teacher liked to linger in the hall for a minute in order to catch the stragglers or potential walk-outs. Since I didn't feel like dealing with the wiry old bat, I darted into the bathroom and teleported from there.

I wound up on the roof, where my hair was thrown back by a gust of wind from the west, sending the briny scent of the ocean to cover the distance that separated it from the high school. Palm trees waved over the grounds, rustling in a way that seemed meant to tease deciduous trees that would soon lose their beauty as autumn crept over the northern hemisphere. After witnessing the verdant existence of Hawaii's wildlife, however, it was a pathetic attempt at superiority.

After releasing a deep breath, I sat on the edge of the building, letting my legs dangle over the side. I allowed my eyes to close for a minute as I begged the drowsiness to strike once more. A quick catnap on the roof would do me good. Of course, so would not having nightmares, not being in California, and not being three thousand miles away from my best friend.

My head snapped from side to side in a quick shake while I tried to dispel the thoughts. If I began to dwell on anything, any chance of salvaging my day would fly away. Considering how many days I had skipped already, I needed at least this one to go half-way decent. For that, I needed my drug to be potent and active. Something my own rabid mind was about to deny me.

It was already too late.

My dizziness had long ago cleared, and the drowsiness could not be recalled. Though I managed to scrape together most of my own natural numbness, it lacked the purity that valerian gave to it. There were fractures and holes in it now that were in danger of allowing my hostility to slink through. And that was an emotion which poisoned all around it. I was a proven hazard when my mood was unstable.

There was but one thing I could do to calm myself and survive the rest of the day. It would take most of my energy, which would cut down on my magick use for the day. But it would be so worth it. For all of the thirty seconds I could manage, it would be worth everything.

I let my eyes drift closed before I whispered, "Nathan."

Nothing around me gave any indication that I had performed a spell of some kind. Yet, when I opened my eyes, I no longer saw the cityscape of Oceanside, California, but instead witnessed several boys charging down a lacrosse field, mesh jerseys claiming each member as part of a separate team. In the middle of the pack, the tallest boy came to a sudden standstill, much to the irritation of his teammates and gym teacher. Yet, his emerald gaze drifted across the sidelines, searching for something. When his eyes met mine, he smiled.

"Lex," he said in a voice as soft as my own had been.

I opened my mouth to let him know that

I was there, and closed it a second later. What good would it do him? He couldn't see me like I could him. Though I'd tried, I couldn't astral project that far. Not yet, anyway.

There was no time, besides. I made the mistake of blinking and found Oceanside spread out before me once more. It was enough to make tears sting my eyes, though I wouldn't allow them to do more than that. Seeing Nathan was like taking a chill-pill. Done when necessary, with the object being to make the rest of the day better. So that was how I took it.

Drained as I was, it took more than the usual amount of power to take me from the rooftop to the bathroom, but it was a necessary sacrifice. After waiting almost half an hour in the corner of the handicap stall, I heard the bell ring at last.

After a boring period of World History, I had a more rewarding gym class. It was the only class where my attendance was consistent. I enjoyed the physical exertion and constant exercise that the class demanded. Since I'd also become more dependent on my teleportation rather than my legs for transportation, it was also one of the few ways in which I kept my body as active as previous years had demanded.

I was less grateful when I learned we would be running all hour. My energy wasn't rebooted enough to get accurate times. Though why I chose to care about something so trivial as my running times amazed even me. It was the one class I attended with some consistency; it didn't have to be the one that I chose to put real effort into.

By the time the class ended, even my gym teacher looked disappointed in me. Shrugging it off, I made my way into the locker room and headed for the showers. Having been outside in the California heat while running on a track circuit, there was no escaping the need of a shower. Of course, it was a short and painless necessity for all of us and I soon found myself slipping into my clothes once more.

"Cool tattoo. Home job?"

I didn't have to turn around to know that it was the girl with the blue tips. Her voice was casual, without being friendly or eager. Instead, there was a hint of familiar apathy to her tone that allowed me to believe she was damaged how I was. No doubt by the suicide of the boy who haunted her.

"Traditional gift from a Hawaiian Elder," I answered while I finished clasping my bra.

"Wish I could talk my dad into that kind of gift," she remarked, and I glanced back in time to see a sardonic twist of her lips.

With a blank expression, I said, "It is easier to ask forgiveness than it is to get permission."

She fought the smile hard. Every time it began to split her face, she forced it back to a semi-scowl. Then it would crawl again. At last, she gave up and turned toward me.

"One military brat did not just quote *Rear Admiral Grace Hopper* at another military brat."

Despite myself, my lips twitched at the irony. "Was there a better choice?"

To be honest, I'd long forgotten that it was the computer programming Naval officer who had first coined the phrase. Never had a quote been more fitting for the circumstances, however. Which allowed another of hers to flow through my mind, 'I've always been more interested in the future than in the past.' None could doubt her wisdom, but it was so much harder to apply to people than the computers she loved.

Shaking her head, the girl said, "I suppose not. The name's Rox, by the way."

"Alex."

We had now run out of things to say to each other, and we were both content with that. Rox–short for Roxanne, I believed–finished gathering her things out of her locker and headed for the door. I finished getting dressed and followed suit. It didn't occur to me until later to tell her how much I liked her hair.

During my English class, I had a chance to say something to her, but I didn't. I got distracted with the open discussion my teacher invoked about Shakespeare's tragedy *Romeo & Juliet*. And if I had been as numb as I wanted, I would never have gone off the way I did in that classroom.

"It is *not* a love story," I growled to myself. The amount of idiots that couldn't comprehend why it was considered a tragedy was beginning to astound me.

"Miss Ryder, do you have something to add?" My teacher seemed too pleased at the thought of me participating in class discussions. This once, I indulged her.

"*Romeo & Juliet* was never intended to be a

love story. It was categorized as a tragedy because two idiots drunk on hormones destroyed two long-standing houses before they ended up killing themselves. Human stupidity. That was the center focus of this tragedy."

"I disagree," remarked one of the girls I was in the midst of judging. "I think you're missing the humanity in it. The drive and passion to do what you can for someone you love. There was a willingness and innocence in the way Romeo and Juliet loved each other."

"Innocence, I will grant you. But the drive and passion you described is an exact consequence of the hormones they were drunk on. That doesn't make them any less stupid, or the results less tragic."

One of the kids in front of me shook his head from side to side before looking at the other girl. "Man, she was jailbait an' he was on the rebound. That's not a hookup worth dyin' for."

I nodded my approval of his common sense before I continued, "Besides that, the real humanity in it was how their relatives reacted." My eyes darted to Rox before I threw out another Grace Hopper quote, "'Humans are allergic to change.'

When something threatens to change their world in an irrevocable way, it threatens everything that exists in the now and forces them to see into a future they are incapable of imagining.

"The Capulets and Montagues embodied that ideal. Their feud had gone on for so long, with such vehemence, that it became a way of life. When the potential bridge of the idiots' relationship was provided, it was demonized. Not so much because of the validity of the feud, but because of the threat posed to the feud itself.

"The change frightened them so much, they were willing to destroy everything so that things could stay the same. And destroyed themselves in the process."

For a moment, there was no reply to my words. Of course, the staunch defender soon rallied. "Aren't you putting too much into a story that says in the beginning that it is about star-crossed lovers?"

"Aren't you doing the same by saying that these two are soulmates when they've known each other for about three days? Tell me, if you had known a guy for three days, would you pretend to die for him? Or actually go through with it?"

"Well, if I met my *soulmate*–"

"You wouldn't know it," Rox interjected, surprising all of us. She didn't react to any of us, but kept staring at the girl. "You wouldn't know it. Not really. Not yet. It doesn't hit you like a blinding flash or light up your world like a firework. Finding your soulmate is more like finding comfort. Like finding a safe place.

"It's not raw passion. It's a soft connection. When you're with them, you're home.

"And yes, if it comes down to it, you would die for them. That's the easy part; deciding that you will be together for all eternity and then attempting to make it happen. What's not easy is living without them. Because *true* love means wanting everything for that person, even if you can't give it to them. Finally, when you become convinced that you can't make them happy, you will do the unthinkable: you'll destroy everything so that they're free to find someone who will. What you don't realize is that you're destroying them more thoroughly than anything else could have done. Because if you can't have your soulmate, then what is really left for you?"

At the end of her tirade, I now knew everything that had happened between her and the ghost that lingered at her side. Had her attempt to set him free left him with what he saw as his only option? Could he have been that stupid? That ignorant? Selfish? It didn't matter, really, since Rox would always blame herself. Even though it could have nothing to do with her.

Judging by the way the ghost-boy turned in front of her desk and lowered himself to eye level with her, this had less to do with her than she realized. There was nothing but pure grief written in his features. The kind of grief that was accompanied by severe amounts of guilt.

"I'm sorry, Rox. I am so sorry. I just... Everything was so screwed up and I... I am so sorry."

My anger flared again, and it took all of the self-control I had not to snap at the ghost. Though I'd encountered a few spirits before–my most famous encounter involved finding the body of Alyssa Rice, a young piano prodigy who went missing in 1922–none of the others had been quite as aware. Or, rather, not as pushy about making contact. Alyssa hadn't even bothered to make her presence in my old Cedar Creek home known until I showed up. The two that followed in her wake had done what this one had at first: drifted along until their stories could be known. Then they were gone.

The pattern was the same here, as I'd come to know it. Rox's ghost-boy had been doing the gliding along in silence bit well enough that I thought I might not have to get involved this time. His shaking off of his 'ghost stance' and trying to communicate almost made me groan. There was no getting out of this now.

Chapter Six

SÉANCE

When I got home from school, I was fuming in silence. It was one thing to get shuffled all over the map as my dad tried to escape my past, but to have to involve myself with some stranger because I had to get rid of another ghost was asking a bit much. Even from my magick.

Rox seemed okay as a person, but I wasn't looking for friends. Between Nathan and Matt, I didn't need to add anyone else to my circle. However, if I was going to resolve her ghost problem, it would require knowing her better. Maybe even getting an alone moment with the ghost boy I'd been ignoring. If he didn't realize I could see him by now, he was going to learn.

My mom took one look at me when I walked

in the door and her brows contracted. "What's wrong?"

Without stopping, I went to my room, growling, "I have to do a séance."

It wasn't that I objected to ghosts offhand. Alyssa Rice had been the whole reason I learned to do what I could. She was the reason I had turned to Morgan and begun to learn magick. For almost three months, it was the scavenger hunt of her memories that helped me identify what happened to her. After her, spirits were kind of my specialty.

I just didn't want to deal with this one. Not an active suicide victim. If what happened to him was as I surmised, the last person he should be talking to was me. He didn't deserve peace. He didn't deserve forgiveness. And he didn't deserve to move on. Not if he thought killing himself was preferable to dealing with his problems.

Yet, Rox deserved to live with her guilt even less. Because of what he did, she was living with the idea that she was the reason. Every day. Instead of blaming him for being an asshole, she was blaming herself for being the reason he killed himself. I couldn't let her live with that.

At least when Morgan left me, it was to save herself. She was already dying, suffering from mild heart attacks for months before she drank her last cup of oleander tea. Her leaving me wasn't so much a matter of choice as it was an inevitability. The decision she made was to end her suffering prematurely. It was meant to give me less heartache, but it didn't. How could it?

No. Ghosts weren't my problem. People who committed suicide were.

I wasn't in the right state of mind for this, but I didn't care. After slamming the door behind me and throwing my bag atop my dresser, I stood in the center of my room while five white candles formed a circle in front of me. Closing my eyes, I focused on the face of the boy, murmuring a calling spell under my breath. It would have worked better if I knew his name, but I was too worked up to go looking for it.

Of course, that's why the spell didn't work. Instead, the flames of the candles were blown out by a small whirl of power that appeared in their center, but no spirit showed up. Disgusted, I let the candles return to their cupboard and I sank to the floor in frustration.

Every witch experienced magick differently. Some had wills strong enough to force it into doing their bidding, but that had a tendency to mean that they were unable to understand it. Others were so meek about their magick, that they did not take charge of it, but put out a simple request for it and waited for it to happen. I was neither of those kinds.

How I was taught was simple: magick could be guided, not controlled. The magick that lived in me was an entity on its own, and it could make or break any witch at any time. Much like those that asked for what they wanted, I made my intentions known to my magick, and let it know that I expected it to do as I wanted. If I had the energy to work it-because that was the price magick demanded-then it gave in.

But magick had its own rules. Besides the use of energy, most spells had to be specific in their intent, manner of execution, and target. It was why DNA was always a wonderful thing to have in working a complicated spell that involved another person.

A séance involved another person and required great mental focus to make contact with the right person. It was why mediums in the 1920s often asked for a personal item of the person who was deceased. The easy way to describe it was like making a phone call: couldn't get ahold of the right person without the phone number. Since I didn't have the name of Rox's spirit follower, there was no guarantee that I could get hold of him and bring him to me.

Since my mind was roiling with irritation and my own prejudice, I knew it was a long shot to experience any type of success with this. Didn't mean I wasn't frustrated at my magick's refusal to cooperate. Of course, I didn't have the necessary energy, either. After my visit with Nathan, I was too drained to try to call a haunting person away from the object of his obsession. Overall, I was frustrated and irritable and my magick was having nothing to do with me.

There were two options I had after that. One: to take a break and let it go for now. Or go on the offensive and look up past newspapers and search the internet for the boy's identity. Though I knew which one I should do, I already knew what I would do. After all, I didn't have anything more pressing to worry about.

These days, very few things surprised my mother more than when I asked for something. Or when I walked around the house, instead of flashing from one room to the other. When I walked into the living room, I found her leaning back into the couch with a textbook in her lap and a cup of coffee growing cold beside her. Seeing her study away for an interior design degree, I felt a bit of pride in her determination.

Though she claimed she wanted a new career, I knew it was because of me that she chose not to teach anymore. Taking online courses allowed her to stay busy while remaining at home. That way she was accessible to me at any time, while making it seem like it was for her benefit. In a lot of ways, it was more for her benefit than she realized. And I was more grateful than I would ever let her know.

Spending a tiny amount of energy to reheat her coffee, I cleared my throat behind her. "Mom? Can I use your computer?"

"Hm? What for?" She flipped a page in her book before looking up at me.

"Research," I answered.

"School?"

I shrugged. She didn't need to know what was going on. Seeing that I wasn't going to give her a straight answer, my mom shrugged.

"Go for it." Then she reached for her cup of coffee. I almost smiled when she realized how warm it was. By the time she turned back, I was gone.

The best part about living in a city versus a small town like Cedar Creek was the fact that the newspapers and reports were online. Cedar Creek probably wouldn't see the need for almost a full decade. Oceanside had done so already. Of course, now I had to figure out if the suicide of a teenager was newsworthy enough to get a mention. If he wasn't, I would have to pick through dozens of obituaries, assuming anyone posted them online. Should that fail me, I would have to go back to the beginning. To Rox.

I got lucky. While his suicide didn't make the city papers, it made the base ones. Gage Alvarez was a military brat like Rox and I. His father had been a Second Lieutenant who left the Marines following his son's suicide. By what the article said, Gage had been depressed for a long time, and this act came as little surprise to those that knew him. Which I doubted.

If there was one thing I had learned about with Morgan, it was that those who were contemplating suicide had a tendency to hide it best from their loved ones. From the people who saw them and spoke to them every day, it was almost easier to hide it. No matter how well I thought I knew Morgan, I'd never suspected that she was even sick. Because she'd known me so well that she knew how to play it all off so that I couldn't even conceive of the reality that existed around me.

Considering that Gage had gone through with it, I was willing to bet that there wasn't a single being in his life who would have suspected what was about to happen. Least of all, Rox. When I had to involve her, I would have to be careful about how I handled it. Which was another reason I didn't want to deal with Gage; I had never had to deal with living people to find out the truth of a ghost's mystery. Rox could either be a source of invaluable information, or she would be a liability and stand in the way of me getting this done.

With a sigh, I deleted the history on my

mother's computer. Now that I knew his name, I would be able to perform a proper séance. When my energy returned, anyway. In the meantime, I had to rest. My impulsive and irritable mood was fading, and it left me with a clearer mind. One that urged me to observe him and Rox a few more times before I made my move.

I still held out a foolish hope that I might not have to get involved.

Chapter Seven

ON THE FLY

I skipped dinner again, preferring the solitude and calm of my room rather than a tense staring contest with my father. When I was hungry, I'd slink out in the middle of the night and fill myself with something quick and easy to fix. My mom always made sure there were things available for me to make in near-silence. Like all moms, she knew even what I didn't want her to.

But she didn't know about this.

My jaw clenched as the ivy leaf began to embed itself in the flesh near my elbow. Tender as it was, I knew there was no hope. I was going to scream. The barrier sprang up around the room just as the shriek erupted from my throat. I hammered my heels against the tile, screaming with every last gasp of breath in me. At last, the burning began to stop and I turned my head to see the new scar that marked the day. It was one of the most painful yet, and my eyes had watered with the experience. The last time that happened was when I'd finished the underside of my arm, near my armpit.

After a minute, when I was sure the shaking was manageable, I pushed myself to my feet and stumbled against the vanity. Unlike other kinds of injuries, burns were some of the most difficult for the body to handle. At this point, my body was not only expelling incredible amounts of energy to deal with my self-mutilation, but having to deal with the same level of trauma every twenty-four hours. In a conscious, self-aware manner, I knew the kind of stress and damage I was doing to myself.

In an even more conscious and aware manner, I knew that I didn't care. The burns were reminders. They were a pattern. A form of therapy for me. When I burned, I was committing this day to memory. Another one that I had survived, despite everything that was going on.

I wasn't suicidal. No matter how bad things

progressed for me, I never had a desire to end my life. I wanted my life. To live it and enjoy it to the fullest possible extent.

My burns weren't a mark of days that I had pushed myself to keep going. They were to mark the days that I was forced to live a life that wasn't mine. The days that my parents had claimed as theirs, and would not allow me to make my own choices and decisions.

They were reminders of the days that I let my parents have their way. Because, in truth, we all knew that I could leave at any time. That I could return to my life, as it was meant to be. Yet, I chose to stay with them. Every day, I was giving them the opportunity to be my parents again. The parents that I needed them to be.

Every day, they failed me.

While going to school was a habit that I was far from fond of, what was even more rare was attending with such a clear mind. When I had mixed my dose of valerian last night, I had chosen to do something far outside of character: I lowered the dosage. A blessing in many forms.

Last night, I woke from the nightmare far sooner than was expected. I wasn't dizzy or drowsy at all, and my antipathy for the existence of most of the human race had subsided by a variety of degrees. Not that I was convinced much of it was going to hold out.

As a numbing agent, the properties of valerian were extraordinary. However, it had always been a booster. Nothing more. On my own, I could generate enough apathy to get me through the day. I would just have to learn to rein my attitude in better.

When I folded myself into the back seat, I kept a careful eye out for Gage. It would figure that the one place I could be sure of confronting him in a somewhat-controlled environment, he would be nowhere around. I didn't want to summon him if I didn't have to, but I supposed the act of it would get me out of at least one of my classes. Though I did consider it necessary to attend my second hour class, since it was the one I sacrificed the most.

In the meantime, I would have to get closer to Rox. If things didn't work according to plan with a séance, then I would need a backup plan.

Not that I had to become her friend or anything, but we could deal with each other from time to time. I could also drop her like a rock if she proved to be too great a hassle.

With that in mind, I made the remark as we were about to step off the bus, "Hey, Rox? I've been meaning to ask, but where did you get your hair done?"

She looked over her shoulder at me and raised her eyebrows. "Thinking of adding some color? It's going to be hard now that you've gone all black, you know. It'll have to be bleached first, and that's a pain in the ass."

I tried to hide how sardonic my smile was. "It shouldn't be too hard to do." In fact, I could take it all out in five seconds and toss it down the nearest drain if I wanted. Then it could start from scratch.

Rox shrugged, giving me an expression like I didn't know what I was getting into. With thinly veiled pride, she remarked, "Well, I wish I could help you, but I did mine myself."

I took her tone as it was meant. She wished to speak no further and I wasn't of a mood to ingratiate myself with her. Shrugging as if it were my loss, I continued on my way without another word. This wasn't going to work if I had to force myself to speak to her. If we were to form any sort of open dialogue, it would have to be her to come to me next time. Though she had begun with my tattoo, there was no getting near her. We'd exchanged compliments, but that looked to be as far as either of us was willing to extend our graciousness.

If Rox and I were ever to hold a running dialogue, I knew it would happen only if one of us knew the truth of the other. As I was almost always reckless with my magick these days, it would take but keen observation to make out the most visible of mine. Her truth, on the other hand, was far simpler to piece together. Of course, if I took the time to scour her thoughts, I would have all of my answers ready and available. But I didn't want to do that to Rox. We all deserved our secrets. The only ones she had that I was after concerned Gage. I might as well get them from him directly.

As it happened, the class I chose to sacrifice was my first hour. I made it to the bathroom on the first floor before closing myself in a stall and fading out. Appearing in my bedroom, I set about preparing for another séance. This time, it would not fail. My magick had recuperated and my energy had not yet suffered depletion. Plus, I had his name. It would be almost impossible for him to resist my call.

Once more, the white pillar candles created a circle on my floor, lighting themselves with very little prompt. Standing before them, I closed my eyes and let the magick form in a steady flow from me to the circle. Then I began the calling spell. It was a simple thing that involved more concentration than anything, though some witches liked to dress it up with Latin chants or incense and ritual gowns. None of it was needed, but it helped some individuals to focus better. I was just one of those lucky ones that didn't need to look or act witchy to aid my work. It was all done, more or less, on the fly for me.

Gage's name was the last word to leave my lips before the magick within the circle started to crackle. Sparks of lightning shot between each of the pillars as it reacted to the changing atmosphere. Storm clouds gathered in heavy, dark curtains within the confines of the candles. In a rush, they were expelled from the room, leaving a ghost in their wake.

"Where...?" Gage muttered as he turned around the room. When he came to face me, his jaw fell open. "You!"

I gave him a bland expression, as I was far from eager to see him again. Yet, I had to let him feel his surprise and react to it. He wasn't like my other encounters, where there had been some acceptance of the facts of life and only the need to have their story told was what caused them to linger. Instead, he was a confused idiot that was far more active than I had experience with. Not that that would let me take things slow.

"You can see me? This whole time?" he demanded after a moment.

I nodded. "Yes, I could see you the whole time."

His eyes widened. For a second, hurt flashed across his face before being replaced by an indignant anger. I almost smiled at the irony. Of the two of us, who had more of a right to be indignant or angry, I wondered.

"Why didn't you say anything?"

I shrugged. "What need was there? You were

going through your process. Every ghost has one, and I don't often need to be involved."

His upper lip curled a little and I almost rolled my eyes at his disgust. Because clearly my life should revolve around helping every dead person I came across resolve their issues.

"Then why am I here? Why not let me keep going through my process?"

I sighed. "Because your process is not going to work out for you in the long run, and it might be half a century before you encounter another being with my skillset. So, I'm going to try to help you get through it at hyper speed."

"Why me?" The fact that he seemed to be trying to outdo me in the irritated department was no longer cute.

"I have no idea," I snapped. "Personally, there are about a dozen other spirits around that I'd rather be working with. At least they're over their 'I'm dead' angst and regret. And they're not haunting a girl I have to see every day."

His indignancy stepped up a notch and he threw his arms out to his sides. "Then why bother helping me at all?"

"Because Rox doesn't deserve to deal with

your ass on a daily basis. Haven't you done enough to her already?"

That hit a nerve. Gage's lips parted and his arms lowered back to his side while he stared at me. Taking the silence that was offered, I laid it all out on the table.

"The truth is, Gage, I couldn't give a damn if you went on existing in your own little purgatory. It doesn't matter to me one little bit. I'm not here for you. I don't even want to see you. And the only reason I am bothering to attempt to help you is because your presence here is going to screw up Rox's life. That's a guarantee. So the sooner you're done with this melodrama you've got going on, the better off all of us will be."

Gage's features twisted with disbelief. "Are you always such a bitch?"

A smile tugged at my lips. "Only to those who deserve it."

"What did I ever do to you?" he demanded.

I looked pointedly at the slashes running up both of his forearms, allowing him to bleed out. Instead of going the route of pills and alcohol, he'd chosen the drawn-out process of bloodletting. The amount of stupidity that had resided in that decision was not something I could fathom.

Raising my eyes to his, I remarked, "Why would you have to do something *to me* for me to find you unworthy? Don't you think what you did to Rox was enough? Do you even understand what you have done?"

His face darkened into a glare. "What happened between me and Rox has nothing to do with you."

"Oh, but it does," I assured him. "Do you see where you are? Don't you understand why I am doing this? It is not because I am given the choice, but because I bear the responsibility. The moment you made your outburst yesterday, you were mine to deal with. So, I will deal with you, and this will be over for all of us. Agreed?"

I rolled my eyes as his lips curled into another sneer. "No. I don't want your help and I don't need it." With that, he attempted to vanish.

'Attempted' being the key word. The magick had locked him in place the moment he arrived. No matter what tricks he had learned in the months following his death, I had many more and of higher quality waiting up my sleeves.

"What's going on? What's happening?" he

growled. Gage took a step toward me, but was confined inside of the circle. His glare hardened and I knew then that he was trying to intimidate me. As if he were worthy to make threats.

"What is happening is that you are now subject to my will. My whims. Try as you might, Gage, it is by my decision whether you stay or go. Anywhere. At any time. Whether you like it or not, I will do what I must to be rid of you. You can either help me in that endeavor, or you can skulk around like an angry child while I go about what I am doing anyway. I've dealt with far more mature spirits than you, and my way is always how it ends. I will summon you again this evening. You have until then to decide."

With that, I released the magick and forced a banishment through the circle. In the blink of an eye, I was alone. With just enough time to make it to my second period.

Chapter Eight

CROWN JEWEL

I was more than a little distracted by the time my English class commenced. Though I was clearer headed than I had any wish to be, it was a relief to have lost all ability to respond to the insipid thoughts of my classmates. For a moment, I thought I caught my teacher's disappointment with my retreat into myself.

With every spirit, there was a reason why they could not move on. For Alyssa Rice, it was less about her murder–for justice had long been done in that regard–than about someone knowing what she was capable of. She was in need of a kindred soul to observe her life in a way that she, alone, knew. So, when I came into her house, she had found the instrument of her release.

After her, there was George Cleary. He was a young boy that I met when I was eleven. It'd taken him some time to get past the confusion of the incidents surrounding his life, so it was that he had been dead almost fifty years before our paths crossed. For George, the obstacle of his crossing over was the mystery of his death. With my gift of psychometry-the ability to see past events by use of an object-it was easy to reveal to him what had happened. Once he was able to remember for himself, George had moved on.

One other followed in George's wake, and he had been harder to handle. Benjamin Carter had been dead over eighty years before he met someone with the skills to help him. Unlike the other two, it was not his story that he was interested in, but the tales of those he left behind. It had been quite the experience to flex my magick to such lengths as I tried to find the objects of his desire. My ability to scry had increased exponentially during the time he had lingered in my shadow.

Yet, the one thing about all of the ghosts I had come to see and be involved with was that they were very limited in their perception of the world. Benjamin, for example, was aware of the passage of time, but he remained unaffected by it. As in, he did not care for the differences in motor vehicles, was not shocked or appalled by the changes in culture, and was not able to identify the music from my childhood compared to the music of his. It was as if he was not involved with the rest of the world, but existed in a realm of his own. His visits with me were perhaps the most direct link he had between both realities.

Alyssa and George seemed to hold the same status. Though Alyssa never spoke to me except to thank me for finding her body, her flickers between one realm and the next were similar to Benjamin's. George, the poor thing, was so confused that I don't think he noticed anything at all around him.

Which is what made Gage so different. He didn't seem to be a part of another realm. Instead, it was as if he were chained in his entirety to this one. Which might have been why his was the most active haunting I'd yet to encounter. Then I had to wonder if it was age or circumstance that allowed for the others to fall into such a state. With the case of Benjamin, I'm almost certain that it had to be age. If I had met him when he had been dead for a few months, would he have been as active as Gage?

Even so, there was no way for me to know. Gage was what I had to work with now, and I knew it would not be easy. Not because of his attitude, but because of my own. As far as I was concerned, he had committed a sin that I could not forgive. There was no excuse valid enough for his actions. None. Not that I would listen if there were, I had to admit. From the moment I saw his scars, my prejudice was set.

Somehow or other, I would have to work around it.

"Alex? The bell rang," announced a voice to my right. Jerking back to reality, I was surprised to find Rox standing above me.

"What?" My eyes scanned the room, finding that we were almost alone as our classmates hurried toward the cafeteria.

"Lunchtime," she remarked with a roll of her eyes.

"Thanks," I muttered as I stood up to follow her. For a moment, she didn't move. Instead, her eyes narrowed in on my face and I was waiting to hear the dreaded 'are you okay?' that everyone said but didn't mean. She didn't say it, and threw a 'shit happens' grin at me in its place.

I was a bit surprised that she had bothered to notify me, much less fall into step beside me as we strode toward the cafeteria. Every few steps, I caught her glancing at me out of the corner of her eye. Which was fine, since I was staring past her every few seconds when Gage appeared on her other side. The glare he directed at me could have been described as murderous. It took everything in me not to shoot a snide smirk at him. Though my attitude was what set us off on this disastrous course, I was certain that his attitude would have been no better during our initial meeting.

"So, I've been thinking about your hair," Rox finally said as we came to the cafeteria.

That was the last thing I expected as I turned my full attention on her. "What about it?"

"I want to try something. And it has the potential to turn out completely and totally awful. Or wonderful. With zero in-between."

A forced smile flickered across my lips. "Is that meant to encourage or discourage me?"

"I'm not sure. It's just an idea I have and the

way your hair is cut is perfect to try out. But I've also never tried anything like it, so I have no idea how it will turn out."

Forcing another smile, I said, "If you want to try it, I'm okay with it. Sometimes a little color is good for you, right?"

She licked her lips in a nervous way, pausing where her piercing should have been. "How do you feel about a lot of color?"

I had very little idea of what I was getting into when I followed Rox home from school. When she first suggested dying my hair for me, I'd thought it would be at her house with a few boxes of cheap dye. Instead, we didn't even get on the school bus. Nodding her head to me, Rox led me away from the school for a few blocks, moving farther into parts of Oceanside I'd never been to. After about twenty minutes of walking, we arrived at this strip mall with a small salon set into one of the corner spaces.

"I thought you said you did your hair your-self?" I asked as we approached the doors.

"I did. But I didn't do it without the best

equipment available to me. The girls here let me practice on them or on mannequins. I'm not so great at cutting yet-except for my own bangs-but as far as coloring goes, I've got a pretty good knack for it."

I could only nod as she pushed open the door, sending a bell into fits at our arrival. It was a crowded place that smelled heavily of hair products and chemicals. Many of the stylists didn't bother to look up from what they were doing, but the girl serving as a kind of receptionist glanced up at us and a wide grin spread across her face.

"I was wonderin' when you was gonna come slinkin' back in here. What you been up to?" she asked as she got up and gave Rox a tight hug. "An' who's this?" To my great surprise, the much-taller woman wrapped an arm around my shoulders, announcing, "My name is Harriet. Pop Rox, there, is like a sistah to me."

"Alex," I said, wishing we could have just had a proper handshake. To say that I was unused to physical contact was a vast understatement. It took all I had not to shove her away from me.

Thankfully, Harriet let go of me and turned an imperious expression on Rox. "So what you in for today? An' where you been for the past week?"

"School just started. I'm not going to ditch the first couple of weeks to come slum it around here." It was the first genuine smile I'd ever seen Rox sport.

"You best not be ditchin' school. I'll get Carys over there to whoop your ass."

A shorter, rounder woman at one of the stations nearest us lifted her head and pretended to scowl at Rox. "What trouble you causing now, Pop Rox?"

"I'm not doing anything. Anyway," she hurried to add, "Alex is going to allow me to use her as a test dummy. So, if you'll excuse us."

Tugging at my sleeve, she led me to a station in the back of the salon that looked equipped with castoffs from the other stylists, but each one seemed like a treasure to Rox. While she had me sit down in a chair, her hands glided over her tools with a reverent precision before she chose the ones she knew would be in use shortly. A moment later, she turned back to me and draped a long, dark covering over my body before tying it in place. With a small adjustment of the radio's volume, she set to work.

For once, I felt as if the movies got it right. All the while I sat in that chair, I grinned in amusement as the stylists and clients traded banter and news across the room. Each one lost in their own little world that somehow connected to everyone else's. For someone who liked to observe but not get involved, it was a kind of therapy. The only thing required of me was not to second guess Rox while she tried to work–okay, and maybe letting the bleach set in almost instantly so that we didn't have to do this over the course of the several days or weeks she predicted. Not that that was an issue. Any mistake she made, I could correct. But I trusted her. The girl had vision.

It wasn't until my hair was almost ready for the washing-out stage that I realized why it felt so comfortable to me. All of the women that worked in this salon had sort of taken Rox under their wing. She was a part of their small family. Becoming more than mentors to her.

This story was so different and so familiar at the same time. Enough to where it ripped a hole in my chest, but I didn't start crying because of it. In a less-than-subtle reminder, the scars on my arm began to flare to life with a temperature spike. The ones on my chest were more acute with the displeasure the memories caused. Guess that's what I got for going light on the valerian.

A while later, I was finally able to see the end result. Rox chewed at her bottom lip–where her snakebites were in full attendance now that we were off school grounds–as she adjusted my bangs once more. With a deep breath, she twisted the chair around so that I could see myself in the mirror.

My mouth fell open. Where once a sheet of black had existed in some remedial layers, now there were flickers of fire spreading out from my scalp. Near the top, the black faded into a deep, dark purple. By centimeters, it lightened into a pink then red color, with some strands streaked through with a dark blue. The red faded into a burnt orange, while on the very bottom layer, it paled further into a light orange and yellow. In a gradual but colorful ombré, my once black hair had been set on fire. And I loved it.

With a grin spread across my face, I asked

Rox, "Tell the truth. Is it better than you expected?"

Her smile was just as infectious. "You are my crown jewel."

Chapter Nine

THREAT

With as long as it took for Rox to finish my hair, it was almost closing time at the salon by the time we left. As we were walking out, Rox got showered with praise while I got the cast-off compliments that came with being a guinea pig. The talent was hers to exploit, so I let her. I was just as impressed with the outcome as her co-workers.

When it came time to pay, however, I was met with opposition.

"Put that away," Carys almost snapped when I pulled out my wallet.

"How much do I owe?" I asked, ignoring her command.

Rox put a hand on my shoulder. "You don't owe anything, Alex. I asked if I could do this, remember? You let me test myself on you with the full knowledge that I could screw this up. There is no debt here."

"Okay, so I won't tip you. But I must owe something for all of the dye, the time, and the use of the equipment," I argued.

"You think we pay her?" Carys snorted. "Pop Rox does what she pleases in her own time. And most of the equipment used was her own. And each of the dyes she used on you was about enough for tips or highlights, per color. It's not enough to worry about charging you for."

"It's enough for me to worry. Please, just let me pay for the dye, at least."

For a minute, I thought I'd have to use my magick to coerce her. In the end, however, she gave a sigh and nodded before ringing me up. After handing over the cash, Rox and I left her second home and continued to walk toward a bus stop.

"How long have you lived in Oceanside?" I asked as we sat down on the waiting bench.

Rox shrugged. "About six years."

"That's a long time to be on the same base."

"My dad's been deployed most of it. And

they've never moved us without him being home for it."

Another pang of memory shot through me. My dad had been deployed only twice in my lifetime, and both times while I was too young to remember. Then he started adding more and more stateside jobs to his resume and they kept leaving him home with us. We were the lucky ones, and I couldn't help but feel guilty for not having the same kind of ordeal as Rox.

With more than a little trepidation, I asked, "Where is he now?"

"He's home now. For about three months. Could be less." She shrugged as she spoke, as if she were so used to him leaving that it was no longer a novelty to have him at home.

"My dad's pretty much stateside for the rest of his career," I admitted. Of course, I didn't tell her how short that was likely to be. Nor could I admit that it was my fault.

Rox nodded and I knew our discussion of our parents was at an end. A moment later, she shifted the topic back to one that was more comfortable for her, but less so for me.

"So, what made you cut your hair in the first

place? Or have you always kept it short?"

Steeling myself for the web of half-truths I was about to spin, I answered, "It used to be almost to my waist. But when we moved to Virginia, I decided that I'd had enough of it. First time in my life that it's been cut like that. Also the first time that I dyed it black."

In an instant, her nose scrunched up in distaste. Then, as if I'd hit 'interrogator mode,' she began to drill me on the brand I'd bought, how I'd applied it, and what steps did I take afterward to keep my hair healthy. All of my answers disappointed her, I knew, but informing her that my magick was the reason my hair wasn't damaged was out of the question. She would just have to keep an eye on the evidence for herself, now that we'd gone to such lengths to beautify my hair.

Giving me a last, heartbroken sigh, Rox led the way onto the bus. Since I was pretty much a novice when it came to public transportation, I relied on her to get us back to the base. In a different setting, we shifted topic once more and began to share our great music loves of the year. The ride went by much faster than I expected and we were soon crossing over onto the base.

Rox and I got off at the stop nearest our houses and I began walking her toward her home. In reality, I was eager for her to be safe in her own house before I took a single step into my bedroom. Without my valerian dose as high as normal, I felt more exhausted instead of less by the events of the day. Though it was a far healthier kind of exhaustion.

I was glad that we didn't make it awkward when we reached the sidewalk in front of her house. Just a quick 'see you tomorrow' on both sides and I kept walking. When I heard her front door close, I stepped into the shadow of a palm tree and vanished.

I reappeared in a war zone.

"Where have you been?" My mother's voice was a low snarl as she rose from my bed. Her movements were as graceful, deliberate, and deadly as a viper's.

After the levity surrounding me from my time in the salon, I was more than taken aback at the hostility pouring out of her. Baffled, I made the mistake of asking, "What's wrong?"

For a moment, she stared at me with an expression devoid of emotion. Then that low, dangerous lilt flashed out at me as she asked, "What's wrong? You were supposed to be home hours ago, Alexandria Ryder. Instead, you never showed up. For hours. And you didn't even see fit to inform me where you were."

"Why are you freaking out? I'm fine. I'm always fine. No one can hurt me, you know that."

In an instant, my mother lunged at me, her hands curled into claws. They were just about to dig into my shoulders and give me a good shake, I knew. Then she stopped with her palm a hairsbreadth from my shirt before she jerked both hands away and stepped back. Fear flashed across her face before she could stop herself, but it was too late.

Vomit worked its way into the back of my throat as I thought about the last time my mother had touched me. And the threat that kept her from committing the same transgression ever again.

"Alexandria Marie Ryder! What is that on your back?" As was usual, she had knocked once on the door before letting herself in without permission. What she saw as a result was her own fault.

Ignoring her, I finished tying my bikini top in place. As I pulled a shirt off the chair beside me, I gave her a flat answer. "My tattoo."

She was across the room in an instant, her hand clamping down on my upper arm as she whirled me around to face her. Her nose was within inches of my own as she growled, "Take it out. I know you can. Pull that ink out of your skin right this second."

"No."

The pressure on my arm tightened and her voice hit a dangerous edge. "Right now," she hissed with slow emphasis.

My eyes raised to hers, finding the fire flaring in spiteful leaps within her blue irises. In comparison, mine were as flat and murky as a New England pond. It was more of a request than a challenge when I answered, "Make me."

They were words I had never said before, though the implication was clear. As were the results. There wasn't a lot my parents challenged me over, because we all knew how it would end. I was powerful enough to get my way in any given circumstance. A fact I was willing to press into her if she didn't back down right away.

"I swear, Alexandria, if you don't take that out of your skin right now, I'll–"

"What?" True curiosity trickled out of me. Daring her to do something about it. Begging her to be my parent. "What will you do?"

Her grip loosened a fraction as the words continued to sink in. Whatever my mother was capable of, I could match it. With that realization came a tiny thread of fear. Of worry. Pity. For herself or for me, I wasn't sure, but the longer she hesitated, the more my own frustration grew.

"You can't think of anything, can you?" I sneered. "You don't know what to do with me. Don't know how to handle me. I certainly can't be controlled. So tell me, Mother, just what punishment do you have in store for someone like me? Will you even try? Or are you too weak to stand against me? Tell me. What can you do? What are you capable of? Tell me. Tell me. Tell me!"

I saw it coming in the tensing of her arm, but I couldn't make myself turn my head as her hand shot across my face in an instinctive slap to shut me up. I think I might have needed it. To prove that I couldn't feel it. To prove to her that it wouldn't affect me. And to ignite that tense air that was like gasoline fumes all throughout the house.

Ignite I did.

I could feel the heat building and gathering just beneath my skin. Like flames eating away at dry tinder, it consumed my body as it sought my mother's intruding hand. Dancing along the scars of my left arm, the flames surged toward the spot where our skin met. Then it flowed from me into her.

She tore her hand away with a scream.

Before she could run from what we'd both done, I stared into her eyes and found my expression growing cold. In a cutting tone, I warned her, "Don't ever touch me again. Ever."

That was the day I'd gotten my tattoo. My mother had avoided so much as brushing against me ever since then. Following the lunge that was bred of the same anger as the slap, she now stared at me with the same horror and fear that I had inspired months ago. In that moment, I'd never regretted that decision more. It was a whole new kind of torment to watch my mother become afraid of me.

Forcing back the urge to vomit, I met my mother's gaze while maintaining a calm expression. In a level voice, I said, "I was getting my hair done. It took longer than I thought it would. I didn't mean to worry you."

"Didn't you?" She managed to scoff without raising her voice above a whisper.

"Of course not. I didn't realize you were waiting on me."

"How could you not? I'm here every day when you come home."

"Maybe you shouldn't be," I countered, my defenses rising. "You should know better than anyone that I can take care of myself. So why worry?"

She barked a sarcastic laugh. "Is it something you think I can turn on and off at will? That's not what being a parent is. It is one hundred percent worrying one hundred percent of the time. Anything else is overlap. You are my daughter, Alexandria. My only child. I will never stop worrying about you. Ever."

Swallowing the lump in my throat, I nodded. "Fine. I'll try to let you know when I'll be late. Now can I go to bed?"

Her jaw set as she debated whether or not to say more. At last, she nodded once and headed to my bedroom door. I missed it when she didn't even stop to wrap me in a hug.

I forced the thought away and was determined to take a heavy dose of valerian. The last thing I needed was to miss a past that would no longer be a part of my future. It was long past time to cut those ties.

It wasn't until after I was nursing a new scar and drowsy with my drug that I remembered that I hadn't summoned Gage. There was always tomorrow.

Chapter Ten

LEGACY

The nightmare faded in slow degrees, the valerian clinging to it even as it had held off its beginning. When I banished it with wakefulness, however, I was pleased to find my head still clouded and full of fog. Today would be drifted through with minimal attention required. I almost smiled at the thought.

After a quick shower, it was still a surprise for me to find my hair flaring with the fiery colors. My hands kept running through it as I dried it faster. When the last drops of water rolled down the back of my neck, I stared at it a moment longer before I headed out to the kitchen.

As it happened, my early night had forced me to rise before normal, thus I found myself standing in the doorway to the kitchen before my dad had the opportunity to make a clean escape. For several awkward moments, we stared at each other as if we didn't know how to react. From experience, I knew that anything said by either one of us would be viewed as an attack by the other. Whatever easy mode of communication we had once possessed with one another, it was too far gone to recall it.

With my valerian in powerful form, I wasn't about to dredge up memories or regrets that would diminish its properties. Instead of saying anything to my parents, I vanished.

It was too early for school to start and the bus wouldn't show up for another thirty minutes, so I reappeared on our roof. Though ours was a one-story house, I could still see over all of the other base houses that lacked a second story. I saw manicured lawns, kept to regulations. Basketball hoops standing beside driveways. The morning joggers complete with headphones to drown out everything else as they enjoyed the solitude of their run. All as it should be in a quiet community.

Why, then, did it feel as if a storm were

churning inside of me? Desperate to have my own sense of 'as it should be' while looking out over my community. As if the dream had yet to let me go, I longed for home. For Cedar Creek and Nathan. Matt, if I could be sure he would still be there when I returned. But it would be a long time before I walked down Old Grove Road again. Years would pass between now and then. Long, painful years.

"So, what are you, anyway?"

I almost jumped as the ghost appeared at my side. If ever there was a test for the fortitude of my drug of choice, irritating spirits were at the top of the list. Closing my eyes, I clung to the numbness.

"I am a witch. A powerful, young witch."

Gage snorted. "My, we are full of ourselves, aren't we?"

"I'm not conceited. Just honest. There are few witches, to my knowledge, that are capable of the things I have done. Fewer yet to have survived my trials. And at such an age."

"You get poetic when you're melancholy, don't you?"

I shrugged my shoulders. "There are worse

times to get poetic, aren't there?"

Beside me, Gage shook his head, his dark hair falling across one eye. "So, what happened last night? Thought you were going to drag me back kicking and screaming?" His tone held a sneer that suggested that I was not as powerful as I claimed.

"I forgot."

I could feel him stiffen at my side. His entire body tensing as he realized that I could forget him. That it did not bother me not to think of his poor plight. Gage was under the impression that he was somehow important. It did not hurt me to set him straight.

"You are such a bitch."

"And you're such a whine ass. Tell me, what makes you think you deserve my time or energy? What makes you so damn special compared to every other dead person I've ever seen? I'm help-ing you because I don't get a choice. Not out of the goodness of my heart."

"Bite me. I don't need you," he snarled.

I snorted. "Then how else are you going to apologize to Rox?"

"What are you talking about?"

"Don't play that game with me. You wouldn't still be here without a reason. Seeing as you are on her heels every day, it doesn't take much of a genius to figure it out. And if we add how your life was ended, there's a whole hell of a lot that you have to be sorry for."

"You know what, screw you." A moment later, he was gone.

A smile tugged at the corner of my lips as I relished in how well the valerian had held up. Much like the conversations I'd had with my teachers, my disinterest and apathy in the face of displeasure seemed to strengthen the staying power.

When the bus was about to pull up in front of my house, I jumped off the roof, giving myself a soft landing on the lawn. As I walked up the aisle to my seat at the back, I was confused for a moment as people began to stare at me. Then I remembered that my hair was now full of fire and I smiled to myself. In the back of the bus, Rox was grinning from ear to ear.

Only in that moment did I regret the high dosage. It would have been nice to feel the triumph of that moment in the way Rox was feeling it. At the same time, it would not have been worth dealing with Gage while having the short fuse of yesterday. There was only so much I was willing to put up with on a daily basis.

As I settled into my seat, I got a puzzled expression from Rox. "Are you okay?"

I forced a smile. "Just tired. I spent a lot of time in front of a mirror." She didn't need to know that it was because I was shaking with pain and exhaustion, rather than my impressive new coloring.

Her grin turned mischievous. "What did your parents think?"

"My dad was dumbfounded and my mother yelled quite a bit." She didn't need to know the full truth of that, either.

Rox looked even more pleased by that, but she allowed me to close my eyes and feign sleep as we continued to pick up the rest of the military brats. At school, we allowed each other to walk alongside, and I knew that Rox was just determined to see the first expressions of anyone who looked at me. And when the first of the faculty caught sight of my hair, we both lifted our chins in silent defiance.

In my first hour psychology class, my teacher took an immediate notice that I knew could mean another after-class discussion was in my future. Thus, I once more blessed my valerian dosage, and I knew my apathy was so thick that nothing would so much as spark my temper.

As predicted, my teacher called me to stay after when the bell rang. I remained in my seat as the other teenagers filed out of the room. When they were gone, I did not approach him at his bidding, but instead made him come to me.

I looked up at him with bland, uncaring eyes as he leaned against the desk in front of mine. Like Rox before him, his first question was, "Are you okay, Alex? You seem distant today, and we missed you in class yesterday."

My response was a shrug that conveyed my disinterest. Then I stared up at him without any curiosity flowing through my veins. All I desired was to continue with my day, and to have it end. This man proved an obstacle at every turn.

"Alex, I think it might be time that I recommend you to see a counselor. Someone to help you better acclimate, perhaps? I know the move you've undertaken must have been a trial, and I was hoping you could adjust given enough time. But I wonder if you are even trying."

A mirthless grin tugged at my lips. "I am not trying. I have no need."

His eyes widened and I wondered at the alarm I saw in them. Then I wondered if my attitude might not be familiar to him. Did Gage make remarks like mine? Could this man not sense the difference in the statements?

Almost as if he were in a hurry to heal me, the teacher crossed the room to his desk and tore a sticky note off the holder. Over the neon pink post-it, he wrote a name and a phone number. The bell rang as he was scribbling away and I had moved to the front of the room by the time he was finished. Before I could leave the classroom, he thrust the note at me.

"Please, Alex, call her if you need to talk. She is a friend of mine and I know she would like to help you. All you have to do is ask for it."

I took the note without looking at it and shoved it in my jeans pocket. His eyes followed me from the classroom, and I was a bit unnerved at the heartbreak I saw in them. A hollowness spread through my chest as I wondered if this was Gage's legacy. Would this man have approached me with such concern if he had not realized that he had failed someone who seemed similar to myself?

Chapter Eleven

BATTLE

When Rox asked me to hang out after school, I said no. I had plans. My mother was waiting for me. None of it a lie, but nor was it any sort of truth. With my valerian still holding its own at the end of the day, the last thing I needed was to be around someone determined to make me feel.

I made the mistake of going straight home.

The house was cloaked in a sort of conspiracy when I got off the bus. A great cloud of trepidation stretched out to envelope me. In greeting or warning, I wasn't sure. But the moment I saw my dad's car in the driveway, I knew that a battle would soon be waged.

Taking a deep breath, I proceeded up the walk, with my eyes glancing at the living room windows every step. It must have been worse than I thought, because my mother didn't peek out of the curtains as I made my approach. Thanks to my father, no doubt.

He staged it well, I do have to admit. The moment the front door closed behind me, I heard the answering machine kick on and the voice of my psychology teacher floated through the dead air to reach me.

"Hello, Mr. and Mrs. Ryder. This is Mr. Middleton calling from Oceanside High School in regards to your daughter, Alexandria Ryder. I took the opportunity to speak with Alex today about possibly taking up some counseling sessions with a Mrs. Roarke. I apologize for not speaking to you about it first, but I hoped that Alex would take the initiative to contact her on her own. However, if there are any questions that you have, I would be happy to answer them."

He ended the call with his phone number. The signal following it was loud and piercing. For a moment, I waited with my back to the front door, wondering if another message would begin, informing my parents of my sketchy attendance. There must have been one, I knew, for my father to be home now and waiting to confront me.

When no other sound broke the silence, I strode into the living room where my parents were watching me like hawks on a hunt.

I almost laughed to see my mother perched on the edge of a chair, looking between my father and I with wide, wary eyes. It was as if she were a forlorn maid waiting to see the outcome of a duel. And while she would always wish that her husband was the victor, she had seen enough of these battles to know that I was capable of standing against him.

There was no preamble of how he hoped I would behave and how much it meant to him that I do good in school and on base. He had learned that those things meant nothing to me. Not anymore. The Ryder Pride I clung to with a ferocity to outshine his own when I was a girl had begun to fade long after I was first called a murderer. Though I still held to it like a dog with an old bone, we all knew that it was not pride that sustained me now, but a battle-weary resistance to change.

Instead, my father looked at me and remarked in an empty tone, "You've been skipping school again. The year has just started."

There was nothing for me to say that he would want to hear, so I said nothing. I did not deny it or tell him that it was but a class a day, and never for a full day. He wouldn't care. I was still shaming him.

"Is it true? Mr. Middleton gave you the name of a counselor to call?" he asked, trying a new tactic.

In response, I pulled the crumpled pink note from my pocket and tossed it on the coffee table between us. My mother snatched it up in a flash, reading the name of Mrs. Roarke and seeing her office number. If we weren't in the middle of a family discussion, I think she might have called her right then.

For a moment, naked pain flashed across my father's face before he forced his calm mask back into place. Then he asked me, "Do you want to call her? Do you need someone else to talk to?"

Even the valerian could not hold up against the flush of rage that washed through me. My hands clenched into fists at my sides and I narrowed my gaze into a hostile glare. While my teeth tried to clench together, I managed to snarl words at my father.

"Do you think I need to talk to someone? Do you think there is anyone who will understand what I have gone through? Anyone who could even pretend? I can't even talk to you and Mom. How is a stranger supposed to know what the hell is going on?"

"You can't, or you won't?" my mother asked in a quiet, careful tone.

"Both," I responded without a lick of remorse. "Always both. You can't understand me, or understand what I have gone through. What I am lacking or how I am filled. It is not in you to understand, so why would I have you try?"

"How do you know we cannot understand, Alexandria? You've never given us a chance."

I snorted. "Isn't it the same for you? It is a two-lane street we walk, but neither of us has ever crossed the road. We can't even agree to meet in the middle. Why should I talk to you? Why should I talk to anyone? No one is capable of helping me."

"How do you know that? You won't let anyone try," she pressed.

"Because you don't even know why I'm broken. You can't even admit that you were the ones to break me."

Across from me, my dad shook his head in a way that suggested his own temper was flaring. "It will always come back to that, won't it? It will always come back to Cedar Creek."

"Yes," I answered. "It will always come back to that. And what you should have done, instead of what you did."

"I did what I should have done," he snarled.

"If that were the case, we wouldn't be here," I shouted back.

"If I hadn't, you would have been tormented every day in that town."

"You don't know what would have happened."

"Don't I? You were fourteen years old when they charged you with *murder* over a *suicide*. That town has been against you for years. What kind of parent would I be if I let you live in that kind of environment?"

"The kind that knows when to take a stand instead of running away," I snapped. "You ran away from a fight that wasn't even yours to be a part of, and you dragged me with you. I was ready to do what you weren't willing to try. And

I can't forgive you for being a coward."

Without another word, I vanished.

I reappeared on my roof, glad that my parents were incapable of sensing my location. If I heard the door open, I could throw a layer of invisibility over me. Though I doubted I would need it. My words had left my father more stunned than anything else I had said in the past year. Not for long, though. Which was why I had made good my escape. It wasn't worth it to hang around when he recovered from being called a coward.

"Is that really what you think of your dad?"

I almost jumped as my head whipped to the side to find Gage studying me. Then his words sank in and my eyes narrowed into a glare. "Were you stalking me?"

Gage shrugged, but I could see the amusement in his eyes. "I don't know if it's called stalking if you don't have much of a choice. Between you and Rox, I'm bounced back and forth. I don't know the reason or how to control it yet, but I'll figure it out."

"Make it quick, and make sure it's not me too often," I grumbled as I turned my gaze away.

"Believe me, I'm working on it. So, what was

that with your dad? Why did you call him a coward?"

I scowled at the shingles beneath my feet. "Because that is what he is."

"Why do you think that?" he prodded.

Shaking my head, I tried to deduce how much he had overheard in my house. Given the amount of time he could have been standing in my living room, there was no idea of what he now knew.

"You gonna avoid the question all day, or you gonna clue me in?" he pressed.

"It's none of your business." My scowl didn't seem to affect him at all.

"Maybe not, but you can't really stop me from eavesdropping, can you?"

I raised my eyebrows. "Want to bet? I can make it so you can't come within ten miles of this house."

His expression became considering. "Can you? Or are you just saying that to dodge the question again?"

It was beginning to bother me how calm he seemed. Compared to when we were snapping at each other, he was a different person in that moment. My eyes narrowed in suspicion as I studied him.

"What all did you hear?"

"Everything after 'two lane street.'"

Which meant he knew about me being on trial for murder at the age of fourteen. He was sidestepping around it as much as he could, but I felt my lungs constrict all the same. Though it was a hard secret to keep, I had managed well enough over the past year.

"You know, Alex, you might want to lay off on your dad. It sounds like he was just trying to protect you."

Rage erupted through my system and I turned a hostile glare on him while locking him in place once more. "Protect me? Is that what it sounds like to you? You think that I am what he's trying to protect? Your father was a Marine. Did it always seem like he was looking out for you, or his own reputation?"

Gage looked truly repentant when I asked about his dad. His eyes lowered before they moved to stare off into the distance. Seeing some far-off location that I had no knowledge of. Then he released a heavy sigh.

"You're wrong. You won't see it now, and maybe you can't, but your dad does care about you. And you are what he is worried about. Just ... don't make any decisions you'll regret before you let yourself realize it, okay?"

My jaw dropped. For a moment, I couldn't believe anyone could be that stupid. After hearing what he did, to be speaking to me in that way...

"Are you freaking serious?" I hissed. "Are *you* trying to talk to me about *regret*? About *life* choices? About *forgiveness*? How the hell do you think you're qualified?"

Something about my words sparked something in him, because when Gage looked at me again, he was glaring. "I'm just trying to help. I know what you're going through."

I barked a sarcastic laugh. "Oh, you do? Please explain. Explain how you grew up with a secret talent that you could tell no one about. A gift your parents could never learn about, because it would mean you risk losing everything. Tell me how your best friend and mentor learned she was *dying*, then chose to *take her own life* on what was supposed to be the happiest day of your life.

Go ahead, Gage. Inform me what it was like to be questioned and investigated for her murder for almost a year. To be held in a Juvenile Detention Center as you waited for trial. And just how did it feel to stand before twelve people every day and listen to someone try to convince them to put you behind bars for the rest of your life? And to add insult to injury, let's talk about your parents ripping you away from the only home you've ever known, because they couldn't understand what you are. Please, Gage, tell me how you know what I am going through. I am dying to have a comrade in all of this."

It was the first time I had revealed so much to another person. To snap and snarl it in a rush that released a great deal of my anger and disgust. With all of it out there, I got a sense of what it meant to have another person-a stranger-know what happened to me. And everyone was wrong; I didn't feel any different for having told someone else.

No one could help me.

Chapter Twelve

RESPECT

For a while, Gage and I sat in silence. My heavy, angry breathing began to calm and I took several deep breaths to help me push back my temper. All the while, Gage sat in a stunned position beside me, not daring to speak or move after hearing my onslaught. When I could trust myself not to reveal anymore, I released the holding spell I'd placed over him.

In a tight voice, I said, "You think you know what I am feeling because you believe I am suicidal. You are under the mistaken impression that I am like you. The truth is that we could be no farther apart. I am not suicidal. I am angry. I am grieving. And I was betrayed by every person who claimed to love me. First by my mentor. Then by my parents.

"I have a life, Gage, that I am not willing to give up. But it is *my* life. It should be mine to rule over as I see fit. The fact that my parents dare to make decisions in *my name* for things that they want... It is unforgivable. Though my dad says he is protecting *me*, he is only protecting himself by dragging me farther from home.

"Do you still think we are anything alike?"

It took him a minute to respond, and I felt him tense as if he expected a blow. "Actually, I think we're more alike than you think."

My eyes closed and I gave him my silent permission to continue. No matter what he said, I would dislike it. He would be wrong on most counts. But I still wanted to know why he thought the way he did.

"Maybe you're not suicidal, but I'm willing to bet you're doing something to cope with the pain. Something that you can control. With a routine attached, maybe. Something that gives you a physical and visual reason to feel all of the pain eating away inside of you each day. I'm pretty sure you know how to deal with pain better than anyone else you've ever met. And you know that no one could hide it better."

A shiver crawled up my spine as he described my calendar. From the scars on my left breast all the way down to my elbow, a faint heat began to build within them, warming my skin. My throat grew dry as I tried not to react to his words. He didn't need to know this, too.

Then he hit where I didn't think even he could go.

"Of course, you could be dulling it, too. Taking something that pushes it all away, and gives you something to hide behind. Drugs. Alcohol. Maybe even some witchy remedy. Something that makes you go so numb that you can't even be angry anymore. You just stop feeling, thinking, or caring."

Power began to lace through my bloodstream as my defenses began to rise. What he said sounded less like it came from experience, and more like it came from observation. And Gage never said *when* he'd begun being shuffled between Rox and I.

"What did you use, then? If you think you're so much like me, what was it that dulled you to the pain? What did you do to control it?" I asked through gritted teeth.

Slowly, as if daring me to deny it, he held out his wrists to me. "You've seen how I tried to control it. How I tried to make it a real wound instead of an imaginary one. What you can't see is the antidepressants that I used to smother it. To try and beat it back and learn what it meant to be happy. But there are people in this world who, no matter what good things are coming to them, cannot be happy. It's like a critical design flaw with a car. While it could run just fine most days, there will be times when you realize that it will never reach the same peak performance as other cars of its class. I'm a flawed design. Doomed to be a shade less than happy whenever there is a reason to be ecstatic."

My chin lifted as I studied him. "Rox thinks of you as her soulmate."

"I am."

Gage said it so simply, with such confidence, that I was struck dumb for a moment. In most situations, when a teenager claimed the role of soulmate, it was hard to believe. How could they know? But when Gage or Rox said it, I believed them. There was no doubt in their voice at all. As if it were so obvious that everyone should be able to know by looking at them. I found it beautiful and disturbing all at the same time.

Then I found myself whispering, "Then why did you leave her?"

His eyes closed and his head hung down so that his hair screened his face from me. "Because I couldn't be happy. Even with her. And she knew it. She could see that I wasn't capable of being happy, no matter how much I wanted to be. No matter how close we came. In the end, I realized that what I was doing to her was unfair. How could I cling to her when she had the chance to have so much more?"

I soon mimicked his drooping head and closed eyes, thinking back to Rox's words in our English class. I'd gotten it wrong. Gage hadn't killed himself because Rox thought she was unworthy and decided to let him go. He'd killed himself because he thought it was the only way he could free her of himself. Because he was so certain that he was unworthy of her, he had destroyed everything. And he never realized that he had destroyed her in the process.

Did he still not know?

For once, I didn't want to tell him. I didn't feel like hurting him more, though I knew he deserved to feel how deep the wounds he created went. At that point, though, it didn't matter. We were both exhausted and drained.

"Maybe you should get back to Rox," I suggested after a while.

"What are you gonna do?"

"I don't know. Something numbing. So, homework probably."

Gage nodded. "See you tomorrow, Alex."

I didn't bother to say anything and he drifted out of sight without another word. For a few more minutes, I lingered atop the roof, soaking in the last of the summer sun. At last, I blinked and transported to my bedroom.

My mother was waiting for me.

She'd been sitting in my desk chair for a while. I knew that because she'd taken the liberty of spreading her own study materials over the table. It was the first time the desk had seen a textbook in about a year. When she realized I was behind her, she twisted in the chair and peered at me with a blank expression.

I knew she was trying to judge my mood,

and so I made it easy for her. Kicking my shoes off in the middle of the room, I went to my bed and laid on my back. Staring up at the ceiling, the walls began to change colors. Black, blue, purple, crimson, emerald, even a burnt orange. It was enough to tell her that I was at the point where I was going to ignore everything I didn't want to deal with.

After a few minutes, she remarked, "I remember when you were so wary about using your magick. You didn't even want to show your dad or I what you could do. Why did you stop being cautious with it?"

"Because I knew it would piss Dad off."

"And how much of what you've done lately is because you were trying to anger him?"

"I don't know." From the corner of my eye, I could see her incredulous expression. With a sigh, I added, "I'm serious. Sometimes it's about making him angry, and other times that's just a side effect. Most days it's just about doing whatever I can to get through the day."

"Lex, you know we're worried about you. Your teachers are, too. Is there something we should know? Does it have to do with your magick or...?" She couldn't say Morgan's name. Nor could I.

Taking a deep breath, I let it out in a heavy exhale. "Mom, what difference would it make if it were one or the other? It won't stop you from worrying. Nor will it stop me from doing what I can. For whatever reason. You know that best of all."

A weight settled in my stomach as our minds both traveled back to that day where she had felt the type of power I could wield. The day she had realized that I was a far different person than the one she imagined me to be. On that day, I'd fractured our relationship beyond any sort of repair.

Her voice was quiet when she answered, "Maybe I don't know that best of all. Maybe that's something only you can be aware of. But I do know this: you are my daughter, and I will love you with every last breath in me. That doesn't mean I will allow you to do whatever it is you desire. No matter what you're capable of, Alexandria, I am still your mother and I will continue to demand the respect I have earned in that position. The same for your father. Are we understood?"

The walls stopped shifting shades. Almost in a whisper, I asked, "And what about the respect that I have earned? Where was that when you made decisions without me? Why did you think it was okay to take me away from everything I loved when there was no reason?"

Her jaw strained as she fought the urge to argue with me. "There was a reason."

"Not a good one. And you'd have known that if you just talked to me about it, instead of making a decision that would destroy us."

My mother stood up beside the desk. She was looking at the books she was organizing when she answered, "We thought it was going to save us, not destroy everything we had."

I kept my voice level as I replied, "You would have known better if you had just asked me."

She was at the door when she sighed, "If I had thought you were capable of saving yourself, I would have. But you'd have been no better off in Cedar Creek than you are here. It's not our location that is driving you mad. It's the grief that you're not dealing with."

She was gone before I could reply. In her

wake, she left the pink sticky-note attached to my desk. It was as close as she would come to imploring me to see a counselor. A wish that would never be granted.

Chapter Thirteen

HEARTSICK

The nightmare was more brutal that night than any I could remember in the past month. From the moment I closed my eyes, I could hear him calling. Insistent, panicked, even a little frustrated. It was one of the few times that I knew Nathan needed to see me even more than I needed to see him.

I screamed his name as I tore off in a sprint. When he answered, it sounded like his voice was coming from everywhere, offering no direction for me to follow. Trying again, I pushed myself even harder, desperate to draw closer to him. When he called again, however, I found I was heading in the opposite direction.

Almost weeping in despair, I twisted on the

ball of my foot and charged toward him. Again and again, we called to each other. Our voices sounded hoarse and torn the more we screamed in the blackness.

Then I saw him. As happened every night, equal measures of joy and dread filled me. Though my sides hurt, my legs ached, and my throat was raw, I pushed my weary body toward him.

"Nathan!"

"Lex!"

Ahead of me, I could see him push his body faster. Our eagerness began to build as we drew closer. We no longer screamed, saving every precious breath for the headlong sprint.

It wasn't enough.

Tears blurred my vision of him the moment I felt it coming. Somewhere in the blackness, walls were slicing through the nothingness. One more choked scream tore out of my throat just before the walls slammed into place, cutting me off from my best friend.

Instead of collapsing where I was, I ran right into it. Sobs racked my body as I pounded against the wall. Between them, I screamed my rage. My defiance.

How dare anything try to come between us? How dare this wall throw itself in our path every night? Did it not know the treachery of its actions? To bar me and Nathan from each other was as great a sin as I could ever imagine.

I threw my anger into that wall with all of the force trapped in my body. When physical force failed, I tried to use my magick. The wall absorbed it as if that was the source of its own power. Instead of weakening it, I'd strengthened my nemesis.

At last, when I could no longer fight, I threw my shoulder against its solid surface and sank to the ground.

I woke up with tears coursing down my face.

Heartsick. It was the only word to describe the feeling that haunted me from the moment I opened my eyes. With every beat of my heart, it felt as if someone was plunging a blade deeper into my chest. I couldn't catch my breath at some points, which triggered great, gasping sobs that I smothered with my pillow.

Though it was only the second Friday of September, I knew that my days of skipping had begun. There was no way I was going to subject myself to further torment when I was already in the midst of a living hell. Not when the hunger for home was so potent that it gnawed on every inch of my body, eating at me from the inside out.

A moment later, I staggered to my feet as the acid in my stomach pitched in a riotous formation. I threw open my door just as my mom prepared to knock. She took one look at my white face and leapt to the side. My magick threw open the bathroom door and raised the toilet seat for me. Right on time. Vomit spewed out of me almost before I could drop to my knees.

After a minute, I flushed the toilet before pushing to my feet. Hunched over the sink, I was busy rinsing my mouth out when I heard my mother dialing the phone, calling my school. She told them that I was staying home. That I had a stomach bug or food poisoning. Something that was making me puke. It didn't matter what she said, I was just grateful that she'd done it.

Not that there was no cost attached.

By the time I had finished brushing my teeth, she was standing outside of the bathroom door. Like a predator in waiting. I had to brace myself as I opened the door to face her.

When I stepped out, she was staring at me with raised eyebrows. "You never get sick," was the first thing she said. It was an acknowledgement of my skills that had her saying the words with the utmost confidence. She was also informing me that she knew that I was not sick now, even though she'd lied to my school officials in order to salvage at least one day of the many that I would miss.

I shook my head. "Bad night. I'm going back to bed."

For now, we left it at that.

Not that it helped me any. Though I crawled back beneath the blankets, my mind refused to quiet. Over and over again, it plagued me with Nathan's voice. His frustration, in particular. That same urgency still filled me whenever I thought of it. It wasn't often that he needed me more than I needed him, and he had reached out the only way he knew how.

But it wasn't the only way that I knew how.

When I had been but a couple hundred miles away from home, it had been simple to throw my astral self into the familiar settings. It wasn't so easy after a year and a half of lost time and the distance of three thousand miles. Nothing was the same as it was before I left. I couldn't even put myself in the cottage Morgan had left me because things had changed to a point where I could no longer envision it properly. Without an idea of the actual setting, it was impossible to direct an astral there.

That didn't stop me from trying. What did stop me was the energy usage. Even as I gathered my power to me, even stealing some of the natural energy that drifted through the air, I found that I still did not harbor enough. At most, I would be able to see him as I had done before, but we would not be able to speak.

When I released the power, it was with tears flowing out of my eyes in a steady, unrelenting river. There was nothing that I could do that would give Nathan the relief that he sought. The worst part was knowing that there was never meant to be.

From the moment I said goodbye to Matt, we

both knew that it was unlikely that we would ever see one another again. When Nathan and I had parted, however, it was with the knowledge that I would come back. To Cedar Creek and to my best friend. It was a promise written in our very souls and sealed by the memories we shared.

Yet, we were also both aware that we would not speak in the intervening time. It was an unspoken law that said the next four years would be for us to endure on our own. Not because we didn't want to talk to each other or be in contact every day, but because some unseen force had pressed against us and told us that it was not to be. In our last moments together, we had known that they would be the last. Nathan and Cedar Creek were as One to me. And I could not have one without the other.

The grief of that settled on my chest, smothering me without leaving a mark. Once more, I was a failure. Powerful enough to banish a ghost-for at least three miles-but not powerful enough to send more than my eyes to a place I yearned for. Though I'd grown and worked my magick to great lengths, I had yet to cross the invisible boundaries it had laid around me. When it came to Nathan, there were a dozen layers I could not pass through.

For the crime of leaving him, that was the greatest penance of all.

A moment later, I felt a desperate desire to see Rox. Though our situations were different, I felt that she could understand better than anyone else could. If any knew what it was like to have someone she loved taken from her by their own hand, she could also understand what it meant to be without her home. After all, that was how she had described Gage.

Wiping my eyes, I kicked free of my blankets while my clothes sprang from the dresser. I grabbed them and headed for the bathroom, hurrying through my shower without much thought for my appearance. Without even drying my hair, I stepped out into the small hallway and once more found my mother hovering nearby.

"Lex? What's going on?" Her voice was quiet, and it almost hid her worry.

Shaking my head, I didn't bother to answer. Then she really shocked me.

Closing her eyes as if the idea pained her beyond belief, she spat out, "Do we have to have the sex talk again?"

I about choked on air. "*What?*"

She still didn't open her eyes, and instead seemed to steel herself for the interrogation she was forcing herself to continue. "Is there a boy I don't know about? Or boys? Or girls? Tell me what I am missing, Alexandria. Have you not exhausted every other option to get back at us?"

Horrified was not a strong enough word for what I felt in that moment. "Mom, I am *fifteen*!"

"And that has never stopped girls from getting pregnant nor taught boys how to use a condom."

"That doesn't apply to me," I almost yelled. My skin was crawling the longer we talked about this.

"Before this past year, I never thought skipping school, tattoos, and piercings would ever apply to you, either. Is it really so great a leap for me to wonder if you've moved onto sex, drugs, or alcohol? Are you that desperate for retribution that you will go to any lengths?"

"No!" My entire body was broadcasting my incredulity. "Mom, no matter how angry I am at you or Dad, I am not going to do things to myself in order to punish you. If I wanted to punish you, I would target you."

Her expression grew stern as she repeated herself, "Piercing. Tattoo. Hair cut. Skipping school."

My jaw set as I stared her down. Then I ticked off on my fingers each one of her points as my responses. "I wanted it. I needed it. I was sick of it. And I can't stand it. None of which were done with any regards to you or Dad."

"So, our anger was just a profitable side effect?" she asked in a dry tone.

I shrugged. "You said it, not me."

"Alex," she sighed.

To forestall the rest of the argument, I finished the inquiry in a hurry. "Mom, I'm a virgin. That is a status I don't plan on changing. Ever. Now can I go?"

"If it's not a boy, then what is it?"

It was my turn to close my eyes. The urge to see Rox was growing, and I could sense a shift in the atmosphere that hinted at Gage checking in. When I opened my eyes, it was to give my mother a hard look.

"I never said it wasn't a boy. It's just not one

you have to worry about. Nor did I say that it wasn't a girl. But you don't want to know about that either. Not really. So just leave me alone and let me do what I need to do in order to feel better." I brushed past her then and headed for the door. As she followed me, I shot over my shoulder, "And I don't partake of drugs or alcohol, either, so you can stop worrying about that, too."

Chapter Fourteen

COMPARE

Rox seemed a little surprised when I took up my usual desk in English, but she gave me a slight smile before she went back to her reading. While part of me settled down at being in her presence, the greater part of me itched to speak with her. To have someone with whom I could compare my life to, even if only for a moment.

A fervor that was cooled when I glanced at her for a moment and realized there was an innocence to her that I could no longer remember. It was in the way she held her shoulders; in the curious tilt of her head; even in the way her lips sometimes moved in response to the words she was reading. All of it told of a mind that knew of one horror done to it. Not dozens.

In some facts, Rox and I were similar. There were other deeds, however, that barred us from ever being quite the same. While her home was in Gage, mine was in Cedar Creek. Her soulmate had taken himself from this world, but she didn't have to watch it. Didn't have to hold him as he died. Though Morgan had left me because of her own inability to stay forever at my side, Gage had left her because he thought she would be better off without him. And, in the end, I still had my home to go back to. Nathan and Cedar Creek were not barred to me the way Gage was now barred to her.

As much as I wanted to find a friend in Rox, I knew we could never be more than allies. A friend was someone who knew every dark part of a person, and still liked them for it. Rox would never know me. And I couldn't remember what it was to be as innocent as her.

By the time my English class drew to a close, I was eager to be gone. I should have stayed at home. There was nothing here that could help me.

"Alex? Are you okay?" Rox asked as we headed toward the door.

For once, I didn't try to sugarcoat the truth, and blurted, "No, I'm not."

"Want to talk about it? Or are you good with just sitting in silence and pretending you're going to be okay while we eat lunch?"

I had to smile, as she wanted. Nodding my head a little, I muttered, "Option two sounds good to me."

Rox smiled a little and walked beside me to the cafeteria. After the revelation I had about our experiences, I knew this was a far better option than attempting a retelling of our life tragedies, all the while comparing who was hurt the most. She lost her soulmate, I knew, and I couldn't compete with that. But she didn't have to stand trial for a suicide or leave everything she loved behind. It was impossible to set our situations side by side and decide who had it worse, but if I opened up to her, I knew we would try.

It must not have been a great day for her, either, because I noticed at lunch that she seemed to hunch in on herself. Bit by bit, she withdrew into her own mind, and I let her go without a fight. I knew how crucial it was to one's own survival to have time to mull things over. Time to wallow. Pain and grief could not be conquered by sheer force of will, but they could be managed with the right amount of grim persistence. Rox was managing.

She kept her own counsel for the rest of the day. Then, as we were headed out to the buses, she put a hand on my arm. "Do you want to walk?"

I nodded and we both turned away from the crowds of kids pushing their way to the queue of buses. It was a fair enough distance from the school to the base, so I had a feeling that we weren't heading home right away. With that thought in mind, I sent a projection back to my house and told my mom that I would be home late.

Rox and I didn't talk as we walked. We kept to our own thoughts as we drifted through the streets while keeping a steady western direction. My chest tightened as I realized that we were going to the beach. No matter that we weren't dressed for it or that the water would be freezing, there was an inevitable draw that called us to it. So we went.

When we were standing on the sands, looking out over the blue horizon, it felt like the entire world stopped. As if we were staring infinity in the face, wondering which speck of it we occupied. There was so much to wonder when the realization hit that we knew nothing at all about anything. If everything was a mystery, could there be any tangible answers?

Of course, I found that I wasn't the only one absorbed in our own mortality when Rox eventually sighed, "Have you ever lost someone, Alex? Someone close to you?"

I didn't look at her, preferring to keep my eyes on the crashing waves. "Several. One dead. Others left behind."

"Friends or relatives?"

"Family of my own making, all of them."

"Do you miss them?"

Gritting my teeth, I said, "Every time I think of them, it feels like I'm being stabbed in the heart."

Rox nodded before murmuring, "Same."

"Friend?" I asked, though I already knew.

I was a little surprised when she admitted, "Soulmate."

I didn't have to pretend that her words knocked the breath out of me. In the same way that Gage had said it, Rox confirmed it. There was a knowledge they both carried in the deepest parts of them that knew, without a shadow of a doubt, that they were soulmates.

Rox took a deep breath and let it out in a slow exhale. Without mentioning his name, she said, "I know it's hard to believe, but I'm telling the truth. I found my soulmate about two years ago. This past summer, I was left one half of a whole."

I had to talk around the lump in my throat. "How?"

"How did I know, or how did it happen?"

"You already told me how you knew in English. I'm asking how you were left behind."

A sad smile drifted over her lips. "Thought I explained it well enough in English, too. Gage committed suicide at the end of last school year."

Heartbreak contorted her features and she hugged herself as if her arms were the only things keeping her together. Maybe they were. I knew my magick was the only reason I was still in one piece. For Rox, I couldn't imagine what it would take to keep her from shutting down.

I didn't say that I was sorry. Didn't give her

empty condolences that most people used as back-up phrases for dealing with things they didn't expect. Nor did I hit her with my shared experiences. Instead, I sat at her side in silence and waited until she was ready to say more.

She didn't.

After a few more minutes sitting and watching the surf, we both got to our feet and began the long walk home. Once more, silence held us together more than our words could ever do. It was more therapeutic than any shrink's sessions, and it was free of charge and frustration. Maybe my instincts about Rox had been because I needed this more than anything.

After I left Rox in front of her door, I decided to walk the rest of the way to my house. Not that I was alone. Gage appeared once we were out of sight of the house. Like Rox and I before him, Gage fell into step with a silence that stretched between us. Unlike the ease of my earlier walk, however, this silence felt heavy with expectation. He was waiting for me to say something, even though I had nothing to say.

The expectation held as we walked through my front door and headed toward my bedroom. In the one corner of the room, I crawled to the head of the bed, grabbed a pillow to hug, and watched him sit on the edge. For a moment, we could only stare at one another.

A few times, Gage opened and closed his mouth as he tried to say something. Explain anything. After talking with Rox, however, there was but one thing that I needed to know.

"Do you regret it?" I murmured into the strained silence.

"This?" he asked in a voice just as quiet, holding out his hands so I could see the deep gashes that traveled up his forearms. My stomach twisted just looking at the rivulets of blood that stained his skin, even in death.

I nodded.

Gage lowered his eyes, staring at his own ruined arms. "You'll hate me if I say 'both.'" He took a deep breath and continued to speak to his hands, not waiting for a reply from me. "Yes, I regret taking my life. But only because of how it's hurt Rox and my dad. I don't regret being dead."

Working some saliva into my mouth, I muttered, "Couldn't you have found a better way?"

"No other way was quick enough."

My head shook from side to side while my stomach revolted. "You saw what is being done to Rox. How can you be okay with what you've done to her?"

He still couldn't meet my gaze as he sighed, "There's no going back, is there? I can't change what happened."

"If you could change it? After seeing how this is affecting her?"

Gage lifted one shoulder and let it drop. "Honestly, I don't know."

Anger flickered to life like a struck match inside of me. "How can you say that?"

"Alex, you don't know what life was like for me. You don't know how *life* affected me. I mean, even with my soulmate I could not be happy. There was nothing in my life that I wanted to stay alive for. And when things hit their lowest point, I decided that I'd had enough. Nothing mattered anymore, and I was tired of being a waste of existence. As far as Rox goes, I figured she would have the chance to move on without me holding her back."

I did my best to keep my anger in check. These were things I needed to know about Gage. It was this information that would tell me how to send him on his way. To leave Rox alone once and for all.

"She will never be free of you. Especially if you are always shadowing her steps. How can she move on when you can't?"

"Am I supposed to want to?"

I sighed. "You are supposed to *want*. Something. Anything. It is our wants and desires that drive us. That keep us moving forward and chasing our ambitions into the sky. Without want, what is there for us?"

"Death." In the way he said it, I knew what it meant to be suicidal. Because Gage said it as a man who did not want anything in life. Or knew that what he wanted could never be achieved, and so he lost all desire to live.

It was the same kind of defeated monotony that had cause Morgan's firstborn daughter, Freyja, to take her own life. The kind of affliction that deemed existence in itself as worthless. Meaningless. Without anything good to come of it.

Freyja had been suicidal because she harbored too much power to be used. She was a leader without followers. A vessel for magick who dared not spill a drop.

And I was pouring mine all over the place.

"What did you want, Gage? Out of everything life had to offer, what did you want most?"

At last, his eyes raised to mine. There was no light in them, however, when he said, "A reason."

Chapter Fifteen

MONOTONY KILLS

Gage and I sat on my bed and talked all the way through dinner and into the night. He told me that it was his lack of purpose that drove him to believe his life held no meaning. That no life held any meaning at all. From the age of twelve, he saw the world as it was, in all of its greedy, vile, degenerative glory, and decided that he wanted no part of it. Like me, he was dragged along in a world he did not like, and forced into a life not of his own making. It was a truth most kids understood all too well.

Even here, there were differences of course. Ones that I pointed out in censure as well as in well-meaning debate. But the one he could never dodge was his age.

"How old were you?"

"Fifteen."

"So young. How could you know that your life wouldn't get any better if you weren't even old enough to decide for yourself how to make it better? You didn't even give yourself a chance."

"Easy enough for you to say. Sometimes, when I look at you, I'm sure that I could have been happy if I had half of your gifts. If I had been as powerful as you, what would my life have been like?"

My eyes slid away from his. "It would have changed nothing." The assurance in my voice was just as deep as what was in his when he spoke of Rox.

Gage sat up straighter. "How do you know?"

Speaking to my hands in my lap, I told him what it meant to hold magick. "You're not the first suicide victim I've had contact with. There were three others before you, though two had far different reasons to take their own lives. One, however, felt as you did. That she was powerless to change anything. Everything about the world the way it is now displeased her. Hurt her. With everything in a balance between foul and fair, she saw only the foul. Until she couldn't stand to see it anymore."

My hand strayed to the locket around my neck that had passed from woman to woman of Morgan's line. Inside, a little clock infused with magick ticked away the seconds. Made a tock for the minutes. And paid a silent homage for the hours that passed by in this world we had created.

It had belonged to Victoria, the daughter of a High Priestess in the Cedar Creek Coven. She was the murderer of Alyssa Rice, her best friend who had turned so dark in her heart that she had to be put down before she could do more than attempt mass murder. Victoria was also the mother of Morgan, my beloved mentor who was raised by a woman who saw the truth of everything.

From Morgan, the locket had been given to Freyja. Her eldest and most powerful daughter. A woman for whom the magick came so easily, who dared not use it in the most influential ways. Morgan had taught her daughters as she had taught me: to be mindful of good or evil magick being worked by our hands, for it would shift the balance of the world if we were not careful. It was a balance Freyja thought she could maintain only by releasing herself from a world which hurt her to reside in. Some souls knew so much of purity, that even the slightest stain pained them. I believed Freyja was one such spirit.

"What happened to the other two?"

For a moment, I nibbled the inside of my cheek, debating how to answer. In the end, I told him the truth. "The first had a hand in her own death, though it was meant to be an execution. She had committed a necessary homicide in her youth, and when the protection of her mother vanished, she was called to account for it. Then she handed over her child to the woman who brought this judgment to her before she added her own voice in the sealing enchantment that would take her to her death.

"The child grew up to be my mentor. She lived a long, full life, despite the fact that she chose to become a hermit after her eldest daughter followed her grandmother into the lake. My mentor thought of life in much the same way as I do. It is not a blessing or a gift, but a state of being that carries with it all of the promise of possibility. Without life, or the ability to make it what we wish, there is no reason. The stories we make of our lives are worth every breath, from romance to tragedy and everything in-between. We have the responsibility to shape our own destinies."

"Why did she commit suicide?" Gage whispered.

Taking a deep breath, I let it out in a heavy sigh. "Because she was dying. She helped her body combat her illness long enough to give me the best summer of my life, until my Ascension stole that from both of us. There was no holding out for her after that. She drank a poison that took her from me, but delivered her from more pain and a gradual death. I have to be grateful for that."

"But you're not."

My lips pressed into a thin line. "I'm not."

"How do you really feel?"

I scowled, resisting the urge to throw a pillow at him. "What are you, my shrink?"

"Nah. Just curious." His eyes dropped to the bedspread before he sighed, "How much does Rox hate me?"

My eyebrows lifted. "You mean, does she hate you in the same way that I do? No, she doesn't. The thing about being the survivor of someone's suicide is that we hate, we blame, and we feel betrayed. But we don't stop loving. Even when we want to. Rox loves you too much to hate you in the way that I can. She'll rationalize the blame and betrayal away because she loves you. I don't. So, I can hit you full blast without a moment's pause. But you already know that I've rationalized Morgan's death to the point where I think I should be grateful that she didn't have to suffer anymore. Death doesn't bother me much, Gage. Motives, however, mean a lot."

He forced a thin-lipped smile. "And are mine still the worthless excuses of a selfish asshole?"

For one long moment, I looked at him. Then I shrugged. "Yeah."

Gage released another sigh. "I undervalue life and overvalue death, I guess."

My room grew more somber as our bid to understand one another drew to a close. Meeting his gaze, I asked him one last time, "Why?"

His answer was the same one he gave me hours ago, and the simplicity of it sent a chill down my spine. "I didn't have a reason not to."

As he faded away to spend the night with Rox, I pondered what that meant. How nothing and no one had been a reason for him to want to live. How, despite having people who loved him, they didn't mean enough for him to want to live. It wasn't that he didn't love them or want to be with them. Just that they weren't enough when compared to his depression. In the end, Gage had made an irreversible decision because he was convinced life would never offer him anything worth living for.

Chapter Sixteen

SHOEBOX

It surprised me, the routine that Rox and I were quick to form in the following weeks. Though we didn't see each other on weekends, we often drifted along beside one another after school each day. A few times we ended up at the salon, where Rox proceeded to do touch-ups for me and experiment on any other soul who liked her coloring techniques. Some convincing was needed, however, to let the stylists know that I wasn't particularly interested in learning their trade secrets. I figured they were trying to turn me into a Pop Rox sidekick.

If we weren't at the salon, Rox and I were down by the water a lot. The ocean worked as a calming agent on both of us. Which was something I was in desperate need of come the beginning of October.

As with almost every day, I missed at least one class. This time, it was my first hour psychology class that I deemed unworthy. More because it was a Monday than anything else. And Mr. Middleton was far too observant on Mondays for me to want to stick around in his direct line of sight.

Instead, I spent the first hour on the school roof, lying on my back in the warm sunshine. It was a nice, calm day. One that promised minimal effort to make the day comfortable. With my eyes closed, I soon found myself drifting.

At first, it was just a flickering of thoughts. Sometimes memories. Then, I began to sink deeper into a state of meditation that bordered on a full-blown trance. In those moments, my mind abandoned me almost entirely.

It soon found its way home.

Before my eyes, my cottage stood in lonely exile. A brisk wind pushed through the trees, setting the oak branches to swaying in one direction, all leaning to the side as if in a choreographed dance. Dead leaves tore themselves from their place and darted between their parent trees in a mocking display. All the while, the scent of rain grew thicker in the air.

A flutter appeared in my chest as I drew in a deep breath. It was as if I was living in that moment, experiencing in full the true beginning of autumn spreading over my home. Heartache warred with a true feeling of contentment as I took a step toward the gate.

Then the steady whir of bicycle tires reached me and my head snapped up and to the right as I tried to identify this intruder. I should have known better, of course. A ghostly smile dashed across my lips as Nathan came into view.

Relief flooded me as I was reassured that this was not a memory. This was happening now, in this moment, and it was a vision I might get away with seeing the entirety of. So long as I played my hand carefully.

Nathan parked his bike against the fence where I had once rested mine on a daily basis. Adjusting his backpack, he headed toward the gate and paused long enough to pat both gargoyles on the head, as was my own habit. With a briskness that came with familiarity, Nathan unlatched the gate and stepped into the garden.

Then he turned on his heel and stared at the ground where the salt line had been blown away by the playful wind.

Without a second thought, he twisted his bag until he could reach a small pocket in the front. From it, he withdrew a sea salt shaker and opened the lid. Nathan spread the salt in a thin line, knowing how futile it was with the wind still whipping by every few minutes. Afterward, he turned to enter the house. Guarding over and maintaining the cottage as I had requested what seemed like a lifetime ago.

Behind him, a long, low meow sounded in query. Nathan looked back over his shoulder at the ash colored cat sitting in the middle of the path. "Yeah, I remembered," he answered with a half-smile.

I drifted along behind him as he headed for the door. At the same time, several cats drifted out of the overgrown, unkempt garden. Grays and tabbies. Orange and striped. Even a fluffy black cat with a gray ombré occurring around his neck, making it look like a lion's mane. In an instant, I wanted to call him Merlin.

All of us followed Nathan into the house,

where I was surprised to find much of the furniture moved around. The rocking chair had been put in a corner close by the cushioned bench. Morgan's armchair had drifted closer to the fireplace, while the coffee table was moved in front of it. Each move done because the lanky teenager I'd left in charge of my house had brought in a worn loveseat that looked like it'd been rescued from a thrift shop.

My lips pursed in mild irritation while Nathan headed toward the kitchen area. This time, he unzipped the large pocket of his backpack and pulled out a bag of dry cat food. Getting into one of the taller cupboards that would have been difficult for me to reach without magick, he pulled down six old bowls that Morgan had used back when there were less cats at her house.

Nathan set the bowls along the wall between the bedroom and kitchen and filled them to the brim. All at once, the twelve cats descended upon it, most not waiting for him to be finished. Giving the felines a disgusted snort, he put the bag of cat food into a cupboard and leaned back against the counter to watch them feast.

"You know, one of these days I'm going to get

a dog. A big, energetic, happy, playful dog that actually shows gratitude once in a while. That is happy to see me for more than gluttony reasons."

The one I thought of as Merlin raised his head and regarded Nathan with a jade-eyed scrutiny, as if he were trying to determine his level of conviction. He must have thought Nathan wouldn't hold to his threat, because he was very nonchalant in his attitude when he returned to eating. My best friend had been challenged by my own Familiar's son. I had to stifle a giggle.

Turning away from the cats, Nathan opened the refrigerator door and pulled out a carton of milk. The minute he opened it, our noses wrinkled in disgust. In an instant, he was checking the date. It must have been a good date, because his next glare was for the refrigerator.

"You've got to be kidding me," he grumbled as he poured the milk down the drain. As he rinsed the clumping mass out of the sink, he said to the cats, "See, that's why only witches ever live in this house. No one else could deal with the upkeep this old shoebox needs on a yearly basis."

As he spoke, he opened the cupboard under the sink and pulled out an old toolbox that I'd never seen before. Then he grabbed hold of the refrigerator and pushed it out of the way before retrieving his flashlight from the box. Stepping behind the fridge, I could hear him grumble to himself about parts he would need, while keeping up a steady complaint about how old it was.

After a minute, he gave up. "Well, hairballs, it's officially dead. No reviving it this time. Guess Lex is going to have to order a new one if she ever wants to live here."

Without thinking about it, I said, "I'll have one sent next week so long as you're going to hook it up."

Nathan stopped cold, his head jerking up to stare at me across the cottage. His eyes met mine even though I knew he couldn't see me. Or maybe he could, in some strange way of his own, because his eyes stayed locked on mine even as I drew closer to him. When the kitchen table was all that stood between us, I murmured, "Promise?"

He nodded. "I promise."

My smile grew sad as I knew that our time was coming to an end. Before I left him, there was one thing I still had to say. "I miss you, Nathan."

It was all gone before he could even open his mouth to respond. And I cried.

A gaping hole formed inside of my chest, and for several long minutes, I couldn't breathe. There was a burning inside of me that was filled with longing, regret, guilt, and an irrational fear. Something born of the nightmare, or which caused it, made me think that every time I saw Nathan, it would be the last. That one day he would disappear from my life forever, and there would be no way to get him back.

Given the depth of my meditation and the emotional onslaught that followed it, I shouldn't have been too surprised when I could feel the magick slinking out of me in strong, purposeful threads. It stretched toward the sky, drifting along on the wind currents until it could reach the blanket of clouds above. They hadn't been there before my trance.

While my mind had been thousands of miles away, my magick had been here and active. By the second, the clouds darkened and thickened, drawing on the moisture in the air as a tempest threatened the city of Oceanside. High up above where it couldn't be seen, lightning flashed and thunder rolled in an ominous warning. Soon, the lightning would descend, and I would once more be in the center of a storm of my own making.

Rising to my feet, I kept my face turned upward. My magick had free rein as it attempted to soothe my hurt. Then the first, fat drops fell from the sky and landed like ice upon my skin. The first drop hit me on the forehead, rolling off to one side and clipping my ear on the way down. A second one landed on my lips a second later. That one lingered.

All at once, the clouds opened up and a great sheet of water fell down over top of me. My eyes squinted closed as I tried to shield them from the downpour, but my arms spread wide in welcome as I kept my face raised to the sky.

Above all else, I needed this. To have something wash clean the guilt, despair, and anguish that came from visiting Nathan. I needed something to cleanse me of my homesickness and heartache. The rain allowed me to breathe.

That was when I came to the most heartbreaking decision I'd ever made: I couldn't see him again. Not like that. No more remote viewing or trance-traveling. I wouldn't even attempt an astral projection.

It was time to let Nathan go. To let Cedar Creek go. If I dwelled on them for the next three years as I had been, it would destroy me. Three years. Once those were up, I would be home once more. Until then, they had to be pushed to the back of my mind, or else I would go mad with grief over them. And Nathan wouldn't want that for me.

At last, my head bowed and I released a last, painful sob. In it went all of my self-pity, reproach, and misery. All of the things I couldn't afford to cling to anymore. And in three years, they would be waiting for me to pick them up again. Of that I had no doubt.

Today, I let it pour.

Chapter Seventeen

PITY

As I'd promised, I dragged Rox to a big box store that afternoon that was sure to have locations on my end of the country. Though Nathan probably wouldn't think much of it, I chose a small refrigerator that was nothing near fancy and had it ordered through the store to be shipped to the house on Old Grove Road. Everyone always looked at me funny when I put that for an address, but a little magick had a tendency to compel them not to say any more about it.

After that, I did my best to close off my past behind that black wall where I hid all of my other memories. Though I'd kept Cedar Creek and Nathan in the foreground for over a year in order to remind myself why I was getting through each day, I couldn't keep them there and keep my sanity. It was time to let go and move on.

Of course, there was no avoiding the questions once we left the store. Rox and I hopped on a bus to take us back to the base, since it took longer to get around than I thought it would. Settling down toward the back of the bus, she turned and raised her eyebrows at me.

"So, why did you buy a fridge?"

There was no way to get around what was coming next. "For my house."

"You have base housing. Kinda required that they take care of the appliances, unless you want an upgrade. And that was not an upgrade."

"It's not for here, Rox. It is for my house," I sighed. "I have a cottage that was willed to me. Yesterday I got in touch with the caretaker and was informed that the refrigerator had died. So, I told him the new one would be there next week."

Rox's jaw hung so low, she could have caught flies with it. I rolled my eyes, not liking the impressed expression. When she started speaking, I closed my eyes and gave a mental groan.

"You have a house? That is *all yours*? And a *caretaker* for it? Why are you even *here*?"

"Because I don't want to go through an emancipation procedure. It wouldn't be fair to my parents."

She nodded as if she understood. Then she glanced askance at me. "Did you get left a pile of money, too?"

That nudged a smile out of me. "In point of fact, I did. What wasn't left in trusts for the grandkids, I got the rest of."

"Explains why you have a checkbook." Rox sighed. "Anything else I should know about you, Miss Moneybags?"

I forced a grin. "Actually, my roots are beginning to show and I could use a touch-up."

Rox smacked my arm with the back of her hand. Which wouldn't have been something to remark upon, if she hadn't hit the fresh burn near my elbow, causing me to bite out a curse and shield the spot with my other hand.

"Shit, I'm sorry Alex. Didn't realize I'd hit you that hard. Did I hit something?"

In an instant, there was a shield up between us as she tried to reach for me. At the same time, I almost snarled, "I'm fine. Just hurt myself last night and it's not healed all the way yet. No big deal."

"I'm sorry," she repeated, looking concerned.

"Don't worry about it," I said again, scouring my brain for a change in topic.

After a minute, Rox looked at me again and tilted her head to the side like a cat. "Alex, can I ask you something?"

"Sure."

"Why do you hang out with me?"

Of everything I was worried she would ask, that wasn't close to what I thought. "What do you mean?"

Her chin lifted and her shoulders straightened, bracing herself for a question I could tell she had to work herself up to asking. "Is this pity friendship or something? Because of Gage?"

It was my turn to catch flies. "You think I'm hanging out with you because of your dead boyfriend?" I dropped my voice into a whisper at the end, so that other people wouldn't overhear. At the same time, I couldn't give her a flat 'no' without it being a partial lie. After all, it was because of Gage that I decided to get to know her. But it wasn't because of him that I kept going places with her. Forcing a smile, I asked, "You think that had more to do with it than the free hair care?"

Rox rolled her eyes. "I'm being serious. If you're just hanging out with me because you think I'm a pathetic little emo chick–"

"Then I'd be a hypocrite. You're not the only one grieving, Rox. I told you I was willed a house and an income. Do you think I wouldn't give them back in a heartbeat if I could just have one hour back? Fifteen minutes?

"Rox, I'm not hanging out with you because I pity you. I'm hanging out with you because at least you know what it means to lose, too. If anything, it's because *I'm* pitiful that I follow you all over the city."

Her face fell a little when I brought up the fact that I had lost someone, too. Which should have warned me where the conversation would go next. At the time, I didn't think about it.

"So, you don't mind hanging around with me? You don't secretly wish that I would just go away?"

"Rox, you are one of the few people in my life who I don't mind spending time with. And if I didn't feel like hanging out, I would tell you.

I wouldn't lead you on like that."

"Thanks," she muttered without meeting my eyes.

"You're welcome. Now stop being weird." My shoulder brushed against hers in a little shove. Rox forced a smile and we lapsed back into silence.

At last, we reached the bus stop on the base and we got off to start walking. That was when she asked. And I felt a fist squeeze my heart a second before the words left her lips.

"Who did you lose?" Her voice was so quiet that it barely reached me.

My mouth grew dry and I had to force an answer. "My best friend."

Rox didn't offer the useless platitudes. Instead, she asked, "How?"

For several long seconds, I was determined not to answer her. Why should she know? What could I tell her with any amount of safety? How could I keep my secrets to myself?

In the end, I fell back on a 'fair's fair' mentality. With a sigh, I said, "She committed suicide."

Rox stopped in the middle of the sidewalk, staring after me as I kept moving. A moment later, she was back at my side, her eyes trained on my lowered face. "Why didn't you tell me? I told you about Gage."

I tried to swallow around the lump in my throat. "It's not something I've been able to deal with a lot. And my past ... it's not something I like to talk about."

"You could have told me, Alex."

"I didn't want to, Rox. That's nothing against you, but I *don't* discuss my past. It's too painful. If I even think about it for too long, it begins to eat me alive. So, I'm going to keep it buried until I turn eighteen and can go home again. Then I'll dig it all back up and deal with it. But not a moment sooner."

"I'm sorry, Alex. Just thought I could help a bit, seeing as I've been through this, too. If you want, we can go on being Suicide's Survivors in silence."

"Suicide's Survivors?" I asked, catching that it was a title.

She shot me a half-apologetic, half-wry smile. "That's what we call ourselves in my support group. Suicide's Survivors. Those who got left behind when life got too hard for someone else."

My eyebrows rose. "You go to a support group?"

She nodded. "Every Saturday night. If you want, you can come with me one weekend."

I hedged. "I'll think about it."

Rox rolled her eyes at me. "You don't have to, Alex. But the offer is there if you ever decide you want it."

Instead of answering, I gave her a quick nod as we stopped in front of her house. Rox gave me one last commiserating smile before she headed to her door. I waited around long enough to see her wave goodbye and head inside. Then Gage appeared at the same time that I disappeared.

Chapter Eighteen

SOULMATES

For the next two months, I kept my doses of valerian heavy. It was such a comforting idea to
just drift through the days and not worry about a
single thing. To not feel every blasted heartache or
guilt trip thrown my way. To be free to disregard
whatever made my emotions stir and flare. If only
I could shut off the thinking portion of my brain
in the same fashion.

Rox didn't bring up Morgan again, and I was
grateful for that. Nor did I spend any Saturday
evenings with her. As far as I was concerned, it
was all well and good for her to find solace and
comfort in the supporting arms of others, but I
wasn't the type that could talk to strangers about
my problems. Even if they had situations similar

to Rox's, none would have any experiences close to mine.

As autumn faded away into winter, it became harder to drift through my life, however. Winter break was on fast approach, and prior to that would be all of the finals for the first semester. And every time it was mentioned in my psychology class, my teacher's eyes found mine. Whether in warning or in commiseration, I wasn't sure.

On the last day of school before winter break, Rox and I decided that we would pay the beach a visit for the last time that year. We wouldn't see each other until the last digit changed, after all. She was going out of town with her dad to see relatives until just before school started back up.

As always seemed to happen when we had the great expanse of ocean spread out before us, our conversations took on a deeper, more solemn topic. Since Gage's birthday had just passed, I wasn't surprised to find that she brought him up. What did surprise me was the tone she used. All the while Rox spoke of Gage, she did it with a loving smile. As if she were at peace with both him and herself. It amazed me.

"You know, I didn't always believe in soulmates. I mean, I kind of thought it was ridiculous to think that there was one person out there specifically meant for you. How was that possible? Why would that person be so important?"

"Then you met Gage?"

"Then I met Gage," Rox sighed. "And the funny thing is, I don't think we ever thought of ourselves as soulmates. At least, I didn't. Not until right about the end."

"What happened?"

"I'm not sure. I just sort of realized one day that there could never be another person who I loved that much. Who I wanted to be with more than him. We fit together so well that it seemed like we were made for each other. So, I started believing. Not that I said anything," she added with a small laugh.

"Who'd believe you, right?" I asked with a knowing smirk and she nodded.

"Yeah, well I wouldn't have believed me either. But I learned something from it. From losing him. Even though I found my soulmate, that doesn't mean that I'm incapable of falling in love with someone else. It just means they're going to have to try harder for my attention.

And being with your soulmate is no guarantee of happiness. Sometimes you're not meant to work out, for whatever reason, and that's okay. I'll get another chance the next go around, I guess."

"You believe in reincarnation?" I asked, curious by this revelation.

She shot me a wry smile. "Don't tell me you haven't picked up on my obvious hopeless romanticism. What is a true love if it doesn't last through ages and lifetimes?"

"I agree." It must have been the way I said it that tipped her off that I was serious. "Though I think we could have dozens of true loves in our lives, I do believe they are stretched out through our many lives."

Her eyebrows rose as she stared at me. "Funny, I didn't peg you for a New Ager."

It was my turn to give her a wry smile. "I'm not. I'm an eclectic assortment of power and pride. I don't need rules or labels. Though if there was one I would lay claim to every time, it is as simple as it is misunderstood. I am a witch."

I watched her expression closely as I made the admission, wondering how she would take it. Surprise crept over her features, and her eyes darted around, as if my spiritual beliefs were somehow restricted under the 'Don't Ask, Don't Tell' policy. Of course, in a way, it was. Even though the Star of David and the cross could be placed on our troops' grave markers, a pentacle was still not allowed. Even if the troops were Wiccans-an actual religion, as opposed to those of us who were merely spiritual.

In much the same way, my beliefs and practices would reflect back on my father. Within the military, that was how it worked. Family was an extension of one's self, and if a man or woman could not command their own family, what business did they have commanding others? Which was why my father's career was falling prey to my wrath, because he cared more about how I made him look than what was going on with me. If those were his priorities, then I could adjust mine in accordance with my own code.

"A witch? Like...?"

"Ever hear of Morgan le Fay?"

"From the King Arthur legends?"

I nodded. "Consider me a disciple. I was taught the old ways, with a profound respect for what I could do. And a powerful knowledge of how to do it."

She thought I was kidding. I could see it in the slight shift of her expression as she tried to hide her cocky amusement. The kind of expression it would be so easy to wipe from her face, but it would mean doing something I had sworn not to do: become a show pony. Also, I had to face the fact that once I opened this door, it could not be closed. Rox would know more about me than I had ever wanted her to, and I didn't know what the consequences of that would be.

The risk was worth more than wounding my pride. Instead of performing a demonstration, I rattled off a number of plants in the old names that I'd had to learn, before explaining to Rox that I had pretty much given her a recipe. I even offered to show her my cauldron and asked her if she wanted to go for a broom ride later. With an amused grin, she shook her head and let it go.

It felt as if I had closed a door forever. Right then, I'd made the decision that Rox would never know who or what I really was. To me, she would always be an ally, but never a friend. I felt a little sad about that.

I was a little surprised when Gage turned up in my room that evening. After he learned how to control the movement between me and Rox, he tended to stick around Rox. Probably because I was so apathetic with the valerian usage that he could never have a decent conversation with me. Of course, he'd been with both of us on the beach earlier, so I shouldn't have been too surprised that he wanted to talk now.

"You know, it almost sounds like she's forgiven you for leaving her," I remarked before he could get into the lecture I knew was coming. "Do you also believe there's another life after this one?"

Gage sat down on the end of my bed, kicking one leg up to stretch out beside mine. "Yeah, I think I do. I mean, what else is there? There's not exactly a pair of golden gates hovering on the horizon for me."

I shrugged. "I think it's different for everyone. The afterlife. Heaven. Hell. Limbo. I think it all depends on your own belief system. If you think you're bound for Hell if you do evil shit, then you'll be roasting for a few decades. If you think you're going to meet your loved ones on the other side of Heaven's gates, you get rest and happiness. Personally, I know I'm bound for another turn at the wheel. Another chance to get my life together in a way that doesn't leave me damaged and angry."

"Why would it matter what we believe? If it was all created in a specific way...?"

Staring at the ceiling, I smiled. "Magick is based on faith. It is the belief that the part of the Gods inside of us is strong enough to do godly work." My eyes drifted to his. "Magick takes its cues from what you believe. Some of us are able to believe like children and are therefore better at making our beliefs manifest. Faith requires the same childlike belief. Which is why I believe there is a Heaven and a Hell, because so many people believe in it that it would become real even if it was not already created. It is how I know I will be reincarnated, because my belief is so pure, that the universe or God or magick-whatever you want to call it-will take its cue from me and make it happen. It's why I believe we all have our own inner Truth, because our beliefs don't allow for us to be wrong. But, again, that's just my belief. Since I'm not dead yet, I suppose there's no way to tell what will really happen to me."

"So, if I believe it will happen, it will? Is that what you're saying?"

I shrugged. "In many cases, where magick is concerned, that is exactly what happens."

His chin raised a little bit higher. "I'll be reincarnated. And Rox and I will meet again."

"With better results," I suggested in a warning tone.

Gage winked at me. "With a happily ever after."

"Good," I said before leaning my head back onto the pillow and closing my eyes.

A second later, he asked, "How come you didn't tell Rox about your powers? The things you can do?"

I released a heavy sigh. "I'm not sure, Gage. It just didn't feel right. If I opened up to her, it would be a betrayal to her. She doesn't need to be any more involved in my life than she already is. It would only damage her in ways she doesn't need to be."

"Alex, I don't think anyone could damage

her as much as I have. But if you and her are friends, I think she deserves to know the truth about you. I mean, what you can do is the coolest shit I've ever seen."

"That's just it Gage, we're not friends. As much as I like Rox and as comforting as it is to hang around with her, we'll never creep into friendship territory. It's not worth it to try. Before too long, my family's going to be out of here again, and then what? I'll drop contact. We won't talk. I'm never going to see her again. And I can't do that to her while knowing that she knows all about me. Rox doesn't need to be my friend, and I don't need to be hers. At this point, we're leaning on each other because we're both damaged. Give it a bit longer and even I will be able to stand on my own two feet."

"I still think you should talk to someone. Even if it's just Rox."

I snorted. "And why do you think that?" I asked, letting the sarcasm fall thick across the syllables.

Gage's eyes shot to my arm, where the long sleeves hid the several burns that had crept down onto my forearm. There had been a few times when he glimpsed the scars, but he had no idea how many there were, or what they looked like. Facts I wanted very much to keep him ignorant of.

"You're never going to stop unless something big happens. When that point hits, you'll decide whether or not to stop or dig a little deeper. I don't want to see you reach that point, Alex."

Slowly, I sat up in my bed, leaning forward so that he would meet my gaze. "When that point hits, Gage, I will choose to stop. Digging deeper won't be an option for me. It never has been. And you know why that is. You know why I could never take my own life."

He shook his head in weary silence. "All it takes is a moment, Alex. Then you could be making the stupidest mistake of your life. By then, it will be too late to take back."

Gage faded out before I had a chance to respond.

Chapter Nineteen

FUTILE

It was too much to hope that I could go a whole break without having to see my dad. In truth, he was probably thinking the same thing. Ever since he told me we were leaving Cedar Creek, a war had begun between the two of us. One neither of us would ever win.

Yet, the following morning, I woke to feel him in the house. On a Saturday, it shouldn't have been odd that he was there, but the fact that he was sitting at the table was. Though he didn't have to go into the center today, he was rigorous in his physical upkeep and usually hit the hiking trails outside of town. Him and my mom were gone almost all day every Saturday, each getting their fill of the other.

This morning, they were both sitting at the kitchen table, talking in voices so low that I couldn't hear them even through our thin walls. It was enough to intrigue me, and I closed my eyes once more. When I opened them, I no longer stared at my ceiling, but found my parents sitting close together at the kitchen table.

My stomach twisted at this familiar scene. It was very much like the secret discussions they thought I'd been unaware of in Cedar Creek. In Virginia. In Hawaii. For some reason, my parents thought that, even now, they could have a private conversation that I wouldn't be aware of. Although, there was evidence enough to support the fact that they might be setting me up, too. It made it easier for them to inform me of things if they let me believe I was eavesdropping on a private conversation. Either way, the results were the same.

"They want to deploy you again? But you haven't been deployed in–"

"Eight years. I know. But ever since the Towers..."

They were deploying everyone for the War on Terror. Though it'd been two years, no progress was being made in this war. People were dying, and nothing was getting done. And as far as I could foresee, there would never be a winner in the Middle East. The conflict was as ongoing as it was futile.

"When?" my mother choked out.

"In the fall, after I renew my contract."

"It runs out this summer, doesn't it?"

"This spring," he corrected. "Mel, I've been thinking about retiring. I've been in for twenty years. Maybe it's about time to get out."

"Why now? Because they're talking about deploying you again?"

His eyes bored into hers and he didn't have to say the words out loud. It was because of me. Twenty years within his beloved military structure, and he thought that I was forcing him to quit. That my behavior was of the kind that wouldn't allow him to advance anymore. I'd gotten my ultimate revenge: I'd ruined my dad's career.

I felt sick. My stomach roiled as the guilt writhed through my body like carnivorous maggots having a feast. Bile rose up into the back of my throat and I clamped down on my airways to force it back where it came from, but it left a taste. All the while, my temperature began to spike, and flames of fury licked through my veins.

This was not the victory I wanted. This was not the stubbornness that equipped every Ryder to be born. Where was our legendary pride, now? How dare he give in when we hadn't even reached the climax of our futile little war? And, once more, my parents were making decisions about me without even bothering to consult me.

Anger beat back the guilt with a tower of flaming fury, and instead of remote viewing, I threw an astral projection at them. Both heads snapped up to meet the astral's gaze. Surprise vanished from both faces, replaced with stoic determination on my father's side. My mother, on the other hand, narrowed her eyes at me before a grim smile tugged at one corner of her lips.

"So, what happens then?" I demanded, not bothering to pretend I didn't overhear everything. "What happens when you quit?"

"We haven't decided," my mother announced.

"Would you even bother to tell me if you did?"

"Of course. Once the decision had been made." Her voice was calm and unaffected as she played my game. Our eyes held together and there was more than a little challenge in each set of matching irises.

My voice couldn't match hers as my fury flickered over it like light over a steel blade. This wasn't fair. There was a dynamic between my father and I that my mother didn't have a part in. Which meant our fighting could go to the very depths of depravity, but there would still be a layer of honor there. That wasn't how my mother fought. If she sunk to my level, she would leave wounds. She would hurt.

"Isn't that how things are always done? Hell, why bother informing me? Just tell me to pack my shit and jump in the car. Or is there another plane involved?" If she was going to hurt me, it was going to be because I'd earned it.

"Language." It wasn't the only warning in her voice. There weren't a lot of days my mom was ready to fight, but this was one of them. If I kept pushing, she would shove right back.

That was fine. I didn't want to fight with her anyway. In a deliberate shift of my gaze, I caught my father's eye. Unlike my mother, he wasn't ready. Not by a long shot. Easy prey.

"Why are you quitting?" I wanted him to say it. To admit that it was because of me.

"I might not be." He was taking lessons from my mother. A normal response would have been to shoot a question back at me. Any other time, it would have been amusing for him to restrain himself when it came to dealing with me.

"Why are you thinking about it?"

"I'm over twenty years in. Shouldn't I be thinking about it?"

"No."

"Why?"

"Because you wouldn't know how to handle civilian life."

His lips quirked into a wry smile. "It's not that different from what I've been doing. Not many Marines see stateside as long as I have."

He had me there. There were very few jobs in the Corps that required a Marine to stay stateside. They weren't called Bulldogs for no reason.

"Different enough. Tell me, Dad, can you live a life without taking orders? Or giving them? Imagine how difficult it would be if you had to say things like: please, thank you, can you, will you, and have a nice day. You don't know what it's like to be a civilian any more than I know what it's like to be average."

"Contrary to how you've been behaving, Alexandria, I grew up with a profound respect for manners. If going back on the way I was raised is all it takes to master civilian life, I will excel at it."

A feral grin pulled at my lips. "As opposed to how I was raised? Where respect for those you live with is something you can pick and choose when to employ? Well, I guess I excel at that, too."

My mother's nostrils flared and her jaw clenched. Soon, she would unload. But not before I did. I would at least earn my wounds.

Returning my attention to my father, I cut him off as he gathered a retort. "Just say it. It shouldn't be so hard. Admit that you're quitting because of me. Tell me that I ruined your life. Your career. Tell me that I am the reason you are giving up everything that you know and affords you any sense of security. Go ahead, Dad. Tell me that I'm doing to you what you did to me."

I could have carved both of their faces from

ice and still not matched the utter motionlessness of their expressions. Several heartbeats passed before my dad's lips parted.

"I won't tell you what isn't true," he answered at last.

"That isn't a denial." The heat had faded from my voice, and I was as cold and domineering as either of them.

"Only to someone who isn't sure of the truth anymore," my mother answered in a low tone. She sounded ... sad. "Let go of the projection, Lex. It's over."

A fist squeezed my heart, though I knew she'd figured it out right away. She was wrong about one thing, however. My eyes turned flat blue, all emotion draining out of them, as I promised, "It's never over. H ow can it be?"

I let the astral fade.

Chapter Twenty

DEALING

My house was very quiet over the course of the break. Not even Gage visited. My father and I kept our distance, and even my run-ins with my mother were rare. On Yule, I vanished from the house without a trace. After a ritual that I made sure lasted most of the day, I returned to my room to find two colored packages sitting on my bed.

The one from my dad was practical: a hat. Since my hair had grown a couple of inches since my last dye, I could see how he might find it humorous to gift me with a cover when I didn't need one. On the opposite spectrum, the gift from my mother was more useful: a valerian plant. This way I could get my own extract without buying out every New Age store in California. Of course, the real question was how she knew which extract had been stinking up the house.

On Christmas day, we all gave a halfhearted attempt at having a decent day. For my mom, that meant most of hers was spent on the phone. Unlike my dad, my mom had a lot of family, though most of it was extended. My dad had been an only child and his parents hadn't lived long enough for me to remember them. Lucky for me, my mom's side of the family hadn't taken too great an interest in the Ryder lineage and so I was left in relative peace. All I had ever needed was my parents; no one else.

My how things had changed.

By the time New Year's Eve rolled around, the three of us were smothered with our own caution. It lingered around us like gasoline fumes. One decent spark and the whole thing would go up in flames. And I was tired of waiting for an excuse to be the match.

In the end, I didn't have a choice. No flares happened in my house, school started back up on the fifth, and we continued in the same existence that bordered on open avoidance. My family was so broken, even duct tape couldn't fix it.

Rox didn't seem like she'd had too grand a time, either. When she got back, she reminded me of the girl I first met more than the one I'd talked about soulmates with. She sat in the back of the bus, her knees drawn up to her chest, and her fingers running through her hair in an absentminded gesture. It pained me a little to see that the tips were no longer blue.

After a couple of days, however, she came back around to talking to me again. Though most of that probably had to do with my hair. After stepping out of the shower in gym class, I let the glamour on it fall in order to catch her attention. Rox freaked.

"Oh my God! All of this happen over break? I swear it grew an inch a day just to spite me," she berated as she ran her fingers through the wet mass. "Oh, this needs to be fixed. Tonight."

"I concur," I said, a half-assed grin working across my face.

For the first time since she got back, Rox seemed to really look at me. I think that was when she realized that I wasn't standing on my own two feet yet. And the break had caused both of us to take more than a little step back.

As if she didn't see how cripplingly pathetic I was, she remarked, "I'm thinking of going deep purple down into a hot pink this go around. Thoughts?"

With a smile, I entered into a one-sided conversation involving style and color with a girl who had all the talent in that area. There was but one stipulation I had when the conversation veered back to my hair: no cutting. If my hair was that determined to grow itself out, than what right did I have to stop it?

Having Rox back, it was almost as if I could manage to keep it together once more. She was a crutch I still couldn't admit I needed, but she was there all the same. Which was why I didn't tell her about my father's thoughts on retiring or warn her that I might move away. I wanted what time I had left with her to be as innocent as two broken hearts could make it.

Perhaps what I wasn't ready or prepared for was Gage to pop back in and start lecturing me on how not to live my life. Because I needed more people for that every day. And it was no help at all having Mr. Middleton try one last hand at soothing the imaginary wounds he thought I had. Though he'd have a heart attack if he knew the kinds of scars I did carry around.

"Miss Ryder, I'd like to see you after school today, if you don't mind," he suggested as he passed me in the hall on Friday. The fact that he asked for after school meant that this was going to take a lot longer than I wanted. But there was no getting out of it.

I nodded in a brisk manner before leaving him behind. During the day, I took time to inform both my mother and Rox about the meeting, letting them know I'd be headed home right afterward. For Rox, that meant no hanging out and I would have a long trip ahead of me. To my mother, that meant I'd be there in a blink of an eye as soon as I could shut him up.

That proved more difficult than I was anticipating.

As the last of his students filtered past me, I lingered in the hallway, sorry to see them go. There was nowhere else I'd rather be less than here. Yet, I had the high hopes that I could get in, shut him down, and walk out in a minimum of five minutes.

Luck nor magick were on my side.

"Miss Ryder, please come in," my nemesis said with a kind smile and sad eyes. By the Gods, was I really that pathetic?

My valerian wasn't at top-notch since I'd been trying to extract my own and doing a fabulous job of butchering the process–I was way out of practice in that department–so a wave of irritation flared through my veins. In that instant, I had a full-blown presentiment that this conversation would end with me snapping at him. Just what I needed: to go off on a teacher.

Entering the room, I took a seat at the desk across from his and waited. The halls were still full of noisy students and the chaos was not helpful to private discourse. Of course, anything we said would be masked by the cacophony, so it was a valid option to jump right into it. Still, there were things I was likely to say that didn't bear repeating.

When the majority of the school seemed clear, I saw Mr. Middleton shoot a glance at the wide-open door. An unspoken rule stated that no door was closed when a single teacher and student were in a room together. It was a sort of security for the teacher, so that the student couldn't claim assault.

The spell I put in place would best be described as a silencing spell. It was the same kind I used to contain my bathroom when I couldn't hold back the screams. Turning my head from the door, I think even Mr. Middleton was aware that my expression meant that I had things covered. In control. Some of the sadness in his eyes was replaced by surprise and curiosity.

"May I call you Alex?"

For a moment, I stared at him with raised eyebrows.

Mr. Middleton passed his tongue over his lips in a nervous gesture, his eyes never meeting mine. That surprised me a bit. I hadn't realized we'd gone primitive and I'd asserted myself into an alpha role. It wasn't often that teachers reacted that way with their students.

After a few seconds, I answered, "I'll make a deal with you, Mr. Middleton. You can call me Alex so long as I can talk to you as I would anyone else, without retaliation."

His eyes glanced up to mine and held for a moment before darting back down to my lips. He was reading the words as they came out of my mouth. It was a learned habit, just as meeting someone's gaze had to be learned.

"Deal."

"Good." I leaned forward over the desk, resting my folded hands on the surface. "May I ask what you wanted to see me for?"

"I'm worried about you, Alex." The sadness flooded his brown eyes once more, making it more potent for the darker tint to them.

"About my grades, attendance, or behavior?" I had a terrible track record with all three.

"While the others concern me, I'm more concerned with your mindset. You never did call Mrs. Roarke."

"She couldn't help me."

"You never gave her a chance to try."

"Mr. Middleton, there are some things you just know in life. Gut instincts. Intuition. Most people have it, but few listen to it. Well, I live by mine. And when you know something deep in your bones, it is truth beyond your imagining. I know that no one can help me. One day, I will have to decide to help myself. And only I will be capable of doing so. Do you understand?"

For a moment, he studied me. Weighed my

words against my tone, watching my facial expression with the knowledge of a man who knew how to soak in the details and come to a correct conclusion ninety percent of the time. Which was why he was worried about me; there was no telling how much pain my face had betrayed over the months I sat in his classroom.

Then he switched tactics. "Alex, last year I had a student who felt much as you do."

"Gage Alvarez. Committed suicide at the end of last school year. Slit his forearms almost to the elbows." My expression turned serious. "He is not me."

My teacher was taken aback at the amount of knowledge I possessed, but I saw it the moment his mind connected my knowledge with my known companionship with Rox. I almost gave him a grim smile. There was no way he could even imagine the truth. For once, I was tempted to tell him, just for the reaction I would get.

"Alex, I knew Gage. He was a decent kid with a good head on his shoulders. Though his appearance was on the edge of extremes, he had his own code. And it was that code that he followed right up until his death. If I'm right, you've got a code, too."

I couldn't deny that one. Yet, there was one thing on it that I could assure him of. "My code calls suicide the coward's way out." It was a crude and not entirely true representation of my beliefs, but it was close enough to why I never felt the urge to do something drastic. I was not a coward. Every part of my life was mine to experience, whether it be good or bad. And I was hell-bent on experiencing everything I could.

"I wish I could believe you, Alex. But, without some kind of help, I'm afraid for your safety. The way you have been behaving is erratic, hostile, and confrontational some days, and despondent and contemptuous every other day. I don't know what to make of it."

I locked onto his gaze and refused to allow him to look away. When I spoke again, my voice was slow and loaded with meaning. "Then I will explain it to you. What you see before you is a teenager who is grieving the loss of someone she loved. The loss of the home that she was meant to stay in forever. The loss of her purpose as she was dragged around the bloody country for no reason except that her past is hard to escape. What you see before you, Mr. Middleton, is a young woman who is *dealing* in the best way she knows how.

"I am not suicidal. And if I was, you would never know. Because those that are pushed to that brink are the greatest liars this world has ever seen.

"You zeroed in on me because I am everything you think Gage should have been. Despondent, angry, hostile, and apathetic. But he wasn't, was he? Gage seemed normal, if a bit detached. He interacted with those he knew on a regular basis, without a hint of the despair lurking within. The few times he let himself crack beneath the depression, he was alone in his room with a razor at his wrists. That was the Gage you thought you should have seen. The one you've deluded your-self into thinking that you could help.

"He is not me.

"I'm not hiding my pain, anger, or distrust. My depression is wide open for the world to stare at. Do you know why? Because I am hurting, and I don't give a damn who knows it. It's not to garner your guilt-ridden sympathy or elicit comments about how I need help. This is how I am *dealing.* And I didn't ask for you to be a part of my process.

"Your guilt is your own, and it has nothing to do with me. You can't help me, Mr. Middleton. You're not capable. Accept that. And let me deal in my own way."

I didn't bother to wait for a response. The spell dissolved and I strode out of the room with my head high. Dramatic exits were my thing, and this one did not disappoint.

Chapter Twenty One

COME CLEAN

It wasn't hard to avoid another conversation with Mr. Middleton. Since the semester had ended before the break, there was a whole school between us most of the day as my first hour class shifted to World Languages where I was studying sign language. Of all the things I needed first thing in the morning, a class with minimal talking was ideal. Why hadn't I thought of that before?

Of course, I faced another strange outcome when I watched Rox grow up before my eyes. Where our shared pain and disgust of the world had bound us together for so long, she was trying to let it go. She wanted to move on. And that was a difference between us that I couldn't handle. At least, not well.

Rox was getting help for her issues. Whatever damage had been done by Gage, she had found other survivors of suicide's sick theft of loved ones. In comparison to mine, it was the kind of wound that compared a burning papercut against a burned arm. Both hurt like hell, but one was far more lethal than the other could ever hope to be. And far easier to heal from.

I never went to the meetings with her. I didn't confide my life's story. Of everything that made up me, Rox learned none of it. Something I was equal parts happy and sad over.

There was an end coming. I'd felt it hit the moment my dad disclosed that he was thinking of retirement. The clock was ticking on our time in Oceanside, and I was hoping to leave as little damage behind me as possible. For once. That meant letting Rox go.

But first things first, I had to deal with Gage.

I didn't know why I had let my responsibilities wane in regards to him. Probably had to do with the valerian apathy, but it might also have been because even he didn't know what to do. I'd thought it would be a simple fix of letting him apologize to Rox. But he wasn't sorry, and she wasn't holding a grudge. And if it was his dad, then that wasn't happening; too far gone for my range of magick to reach him.

Right as February was beginning to start, we both ended up sitting at opposite ends of my bed and I leveled him with an irritated gaze. "Okay, what is the point of me befriending Rox and having whine sessions with you every week if I can't figure out how to send you on your way?"

Gage shrugged, unimpressed with my lack of professionalism. "Don't know. What usually happens in these situations?"

It was my turn to shrug. "I learn. I've got this ability known as psychometry. It allows me to touch objects and basically see certain moments of their existence, in relation to the person I want to know about. In a normal situation, I would just track down some of their objects and learn the story. Then I would know what to do from there.

"With you, that's unnecessary. You can tell me the whole story. Rox can fill in most of the blanks. I know what's wrong with you, but there seems to be nothing to do about it. Why are you here?" The last came out in an exasperated sigh.

For several heartbeats, Gage didn't look at me. He stared at the ghostly imprints of his slit wrists and nibbled on his bottom lip where a couple of piercings once adorned the flesh. There was something he didn't want to tell me. I made him.

"Spit it out, Gage. You may have all of eternity, but I do not."

With a heavy sigh, he looked up at me. "Did you ever stop to think, Alex, that maybe you're not supposed to help me? I mean, isn't it just as likely that maybe I'm here to help *you*?"

I was struck dumb. Could he really be that stupid? Or did he just have that big a hero complex? For a moment, my emotions roared between waves of incredulity and hilarity. Incredulity won.

"You're serious? You think you have been lingering around this place for almost a year because I might happen upon you and need your soothing talks about how to stop screwing up my life? Think about it for a moment and see if you come to the same conclusion."

"I have thought about it. A lot. And I know what I did hurt people. I understand that it was my own desire to stop hurting that hurt others. But if I was being punished for that decision, wouldn't I still be hurting? Wouldn't I be trying to find a way to make amends? Instead, I get to be there and watch Rox grow into a better person without me by her side. I have hope, Alex, that I never had before. I'm okay with what I did, and Rox is getting to that point. The only one not okay here is you. So maybe you're the one that needs a little help."

My head shook from side to side in stubborn denial. "You don't get it. Gage, whatever's keeping you, it's because of *you*. It has nothing to do with those you left behind or even those you come across. Death is the most personal thing we must all face. More personal even than life itself. Unlike most people, you chose the manner, the time, place, and motive of your death.

"If something is holding you here, it is because your entire *soul* believes you're not finished yet. I don't know what made you decide that being the one person to help me was your calling, but I promise you it's not. Something has made you stay here from the beginning. That something was never me."

"So, what is it then?" he growled in exasperation. "What else am I so desperate to do with this half-assed existence then?"

"You tell me."

Gage shot me one more disgusted look before he faded out. It was no loss. He'd be back. And we would have the same conversation again. As many times as needed before he finally burst with the irritation and said aloud the thing that kept his soul chained to Rox and I. Until then, I could go on with my own half-assed existence and not lose any sleep over it.

It was Valentine's Day before Gage appeared in my bedroom one last time. I knew it was the last time because the look on his face was nothing short of haunted. If ghosts could vomit, he'd have been doubled over and emptying his guts on my bedroom floor.

He'd finally figured out how to help himself. Somehow, I wondered if it would be too late. After a year of dragging his feet, and Rox moving on so well, I knew this wasn't a good time. Still, we had to try.

"What is it?"

He started rambling. "Y'know, I didn't think you were right. About me having to figure it out myself. Figure out why I thought I needed to stay. I honestly thought that helping you was as good a chance as I was going to get for sticking around here doing nothing. If I could help at least one person, that'd be worth no one being able to help me, wouldn't it?"

His words crushed the air from my lungs. That was it, wasn't it? The similarity that bound us together despite the fact that we were horrendous little shits to each other. It was our inability to be helped. Like me, Gage had learned that he had to help himself, and no one could do it for him. I just wasn't sure I was ready for him to have figured it out.

I slammed that thought behind the black wall and stood up from the bed. "Tell me," I demanded in a harsher voice than I'd intended.

"It was never you. It was always Rox."

Even I could have told him that. There was a reason his spirit had attached itself to her. He just had to face facts. Yet, hearing the words, I felt ice slide down my spine.

"What about Rox? What happened, Gage? What do you have to help her with?"

His gaze hit me hard and I almost took a step back. "What was it you said to Mr. Middleton? People that close to the edge are the world's best liars. Rox has been playing it up for a while now, but she's not okay. Not by a long shot. And if we don't do something about it, she might make my mistakes."

I felt like collapsing. Again. It had happened to me *again*. I got close to someone, and even kept them on the edge of my insanity, and still I had overlooked the signs and symptoms. How could I miss that? How did my empathy not pick up on anything from her?

That was the first time that I realized my magick wasn't working how it was supposed to. When I had Ascended, I knew to a horrific extent just how powerful I was. That 'impossible' was no longer in my vocabulary. I'd had the ability to move literal mountains with a blink of my eye.

Yet I couldn't check in on Nathan longer than a few seconds. I couldn't tell Rox's depression from my own. And if I got moody enough, my magick pulled in thunderstorms volatile enough to cause a flash flood.

I was so damaged that even my magick had put me on a tight leash. As a result, everything was going to hell and back.

"What do you want me to do?" I snapped at Gage, angry at myself, the universe, Rox, and him all at once. What I wouldn't give not to have to deal with this.

Gage stepped close enough to look down on me. In a flat, level voice, he announced, "I want you to show her your scars. I want her to show you hers. I want you to tell her... I made a mistake, and I would give anything not watch her make it too. Come clean to her, Alex. That's what I want."

Chapter Twenty Two

HERO

It was the first time I'd ever seen Rox on a Saturday. Bitter cold pierced through my coat as I marched up to her front door and knocked. I already knew that her dad and stepmom were gone, via Gage's superior spying skills. There was no getting out of this, for either her or me.

The front door opened and Rox stood in front of me in flannel pajamas, her body holding all of her weight on one side. She looked nervous and more than a little spooked. "Alex? What are you doing here?"

I almost couldn't say the words. "Can I come in? There's something I need to show you."

Her eyes shot to my hair and I almost snorted. As if that wasn't the least of my worries. She didn't know it, but I could sense the blood that she had under the gauze pressed to her thigh.

"Now's not really a good time."

Something in my expression must have let her know that I wasn't in the mood to be side-stepped. The fact that I was showing up on a Saturday should have been enough to tip her off. In the case that it didn't, I invoked a name that I knew would drop her guard.

"Can I ask you about Suicide's Survivors?"

She stepped back to allow me entrance, half-hiding behind the door. Too late. I saw the flash of panic in her eyes.

When she closed the door behind me, she shifted from foot to foot, wondering what kind of hospitality to offer an unwelcome guest who was inching too close to her secrets. It didn't matter, I didn't feel very hospitable either. With a quick glance at her, then at the stairs, I suggested that we go to her room. She was off like a shot.

The moment the door closed behind us, I put a shield up around the room. This was more than my noise-blocking bubble, but more like an impenetrable fish bowl. No one was getting in or out while my magick was up. At least that still worked right.

Before Rox had a chance to notice, I stripped out of my coat and sweatshirt to reveal the tanktop I wore. As every nerve in my body constricted, I let the glamour over my left arm fade away. If I was forced to do this, the band-aid would have to be ripped off without a lick of doubt to maneuver in her brain.

When all of my scars were revealed–a total of five hundred and seventy-eight–Rox gasped and backed into the door. For several long minutes, I waited. She was breathing in short, shallow gasps as her brain tried to process what I'd just done. My brain was doing the same thing.

At last, the silence broke. "What are those?"

My stare was flat as I answered, "A more artistic version of the lines across your thighs. They're a garden of scars. My calendar. Each one marks a twenty-four-hour period that I have been away from my home. Away from the people that I love. Every one is a reminder of the time that was stolen from me. All because one woman thought it was okay to take her life and leave me in limbo."

It took hours to convince Rox of the truth. As far as my magick went, it was easy enough to prove. The scars, in an ironic twist of events, were harder for her to contemplate. Mostly, how did so many fit on my arm? Of course, the answer to that was evident in the size of the leaves and how many of them overlapped. My arm looked like a true, overgrown surface, with leaves being layered overtop of leaves until there was a wall of white a few shades paler than my skin.

After I had convinced her of my witch status and my mentally-screwed-up status, there was one more tidbit of information I needed her to digest before we got into the real reason for my visit. It proved to be the most strenuous topic of all. Again, I ripped off the bandage.

"Rox, I'm a Medium, which means I can see and communicate with the dead. From the moment I first saw you, I also saw Gage. He's been shadowing you since his death."

I gave her a few minutes to let that sink in. Hearing that her dead soulmate had been with her the entire time would have been enough to send anyone into a stunned stupor. The fact that

she hadn't fainted yet was a mark of her character, though I worried that this would push it.

"Gage...?"

"Has been with you since his death." Clear
and clinical. Like her sanity depended on it.

"Why?"

If Gage had been in the room, I'd have given
him a withering stare. "Because he has a hero
complex. He feels like he needs to save people. To
help those nobody else can. He's still under the
delusion that he's capable of it, even when they
don't want to help themselves. It's why he asked
me to come."

"Why? What is going on here, Alex?"

I swallowed hard. "I showed you my scars,
Rox. Show me yours."

Her face paled and her eyes shot to the floor.
A few heartbeats later, she dropped her pajama
bottoms to reveal a wide, white gauze pad taped
to her thigh. Blood was soaking through it in
three places. There was no telling how many
more she'd have been through if I hadn't arrived
when I did.

Raising my eyes to her face once more, I let
her see the damage done to me. "Gage thought

that you could help me, and I could help you. He doesn't understand that we both have to make the conscious decision to help ourselves, or any aid given to us by anyone else will hit a brick wall. For so long, he was waiting for someone to rescue him. After you arrived, he thought he might have found his hero. When he realized that he'd put too much expectation on you to help him, it crushed him. That's what killed him, more than anything."

"How can you say that?" she whispered, horrified that I might blame Gage for his own suicide. As if there were anyone else to blame.

"Because it is true. Gage wants to save us from ourselves, and offers us both as the antidote to each other's suffering. He doesn't understand that it isn't possible. That you and I will only recover when we choose to. You can't help me, Rox. And I can't help you. Now you need to tell Gage that, once and for all. Otherwise, he'll never move on. Nor will you."

Her face had grown even more pale as I spoke and part of me wondered if she would faint. Through a dry throat, she murmured, "I don't know what to say. Or do. Alex, I don't understand what is going on here."

She was fifteen years old, scared, and just had a bomb of supernatural proportions dropped on her head. I tried to understand that as I motioned her to sit beside me on the bed. Tried to picture the fear and shock ripping through her as I chose my words. All the while, I was cursing Gage's name, because this was the exact conversation and reaction I'd been trying to avoid.

"I don't know how to explain it in any better way, Rox. I wish I did. The fact of the matter is that Gage is sticking around because he wants to be your hero. When he figured out that the only way to help you was through me, he pulled a few mystical strings of his own. Now here I am.

"But I'm damaged goods too, Rox. And I know that I'm not ready to be healed yet. I don't think you are, either. Yet, Gage is terrified that you'll choose his fate."

She stared at her hands in her lap as she sniffled, "Is that such a bad thing?"

My hand shot out of its own volition, grabbing her chin and twisting her head so hard that I heard her neck crack. I directed her gaze to my upheld arm while trying to contain my rage.

"Look at me, Rox. Tell me it's not that bad," I said in a quiet, deadly tone. "My mentor didn't decide to commit suicide because life was too hard. Because her eldest daughter drowned herself. Or because her two other children disowned her and told her grandchildren that she was dead. If there was a reason to commit suicide, she'd have had plenty. But she didn't.

"Instead, she suffered through a few heart attacks before realizing that she was dying. So, she fought it. For months. Until I was ready and able to take my power as my own. Then, and only then, did she decide that it was time. That she could let go of the world in a manner of her own choosing. My mentor didn't choose to take her own life until she was sure I would hold her as she slipped away.

"Look at me, Rox. Tell me it's not that bad. Tell me that you could handle leaving your dad behind like Gage did. Tell me that there aren't people that care about you more than you think they should. Tell me that it will be worth it so long as you can see him again. I dare you."

A stubborn gleam set into her eyes, and I could tell she thought I didn't understand. That

I couldn't, because I was so dead-set against suicide. She was right. I was anything but neutral
on this point. In some ways, however, she was
also very, very wrong.

"I'm glad my mentor took her own life," I
forced out between my teeth.

It wasn't a lie, though I felt like a traitor to
my cause for admitting it. I didn't want it to be
true, but I understood it too well to think that it
wasn't okay. If I had gotten to the point Morgan
did, I would have done the same. So how could I
condemn her for it?

"I believe in assisted suicide. I believe that
if you are going to die, you have the right to go
out as you wish. If you can't fight your battles
anymore or your own mind and body betray you,
you've got every right to shut it all down. That's
my honest opinion."

"But you just said…"

"Let me finish. I said I believe in suicide as
long as you're dying. What I do not believe in
is committing suicide because life hurts. Life is
always going to hurt. It's going to be a giant damn
suckfest and there's nothing we can do about it.
Except decide what we allow to hurt us.

"I let my mentor's death hurt me. I let her suicide hurt me. I let being taken away from my home hurt me. *I allow that.* I allow that because I'm not strong enough yet to decide to live without that hurt. That hurt is comfortable to me, right now. More comfortable than warm hugs from my parents, or curling up and crying with a carton of ice cream. This pain is comfortable because it's familiar, and I know how to deal with it. I don't know how to deal with moving on, so I don't.

"You're in the same position as me, I can see it in your eyes. And that's okay. It's okay to hurt, and to be comfortable hurting. But what's not okay is how either of us is handling it. Every day I look at my arm, I'm filled with shame. An all-consuming shame that lets me know that I have failed every single person who has ever been in my life. By the time midnight rolls around, however, I find that I have to mark the day. Because it's one more I survived even with all of that shame burning me alive.

"Why do you cut, Rox? And who would you be ashamed to tell?"

Silence fell thick into the room and I knew I would never get an answer. There was relief in controlling pain. She cut herself so that she could feel that she controlled some of what was happening to her. Some of what was hurting her.

I'd just told her that the emotions warring inside of her were also her decision. And I knew she wouldn't believe me. If I didn't know it was true deep in my soul, I wouldn't have believed me either. But I'd known for a long time that I could make the decision to stop hurting, and I would. Not yet, but someday. For now, I wasn't ready to let go of the comfort of hurting. This was familiar to me; what came after it wasn't. After trading in familiar safety for hostile and different, I stuck with what was familiar. Damn the cost.

I got to my feet, put the glamour back over my arm, and shrugged into my jacket and coat. Turning to look at her, I gave her my most commiserating smile.

"You have to deal with it in your own way. That doesn't mean it's okay, but you've got to know your limits. Trust me, Gage doesn't want you to end up like him. That's why he did all this. He gave up everything in the hopes that he could save you. Just think about letting him."

I wouldn't hear from Rox again. Not for a while. For the first time since the break ended, I was okay with it being that way. We no longer needed to use each other as a crutch. Hopefully that would be enough.

Chapter Twenty Three

LIGHTHOUSE

I didn't take the bus to school anymore. Hopping between my bedroom to the roof of the building, I waited there until the first bell rang. Then I dropped into a bathroom and headed to class from there. No one noticed.

It wasn't that I was avoiding Rox, but I was giving her a lot of space. Time would tell whether or not she took my advice. And Gage would tell me if things got truly dire with her situation. Without that incentive, I left her be. It was time for her to sink or swim, and I could no longer help her choose.

Her choice was made before February was out. Gage appeared on the twenty-ninth and decided that Rox didn't need him to look out for her anymore. He thanked me for what I'd done and said that she had asked her dad to put her in counseling. She was getting help and healing. It was all we could ask for.

Gage moved on that night. Wherever he went, I knew he'd be waiting for her. I also knew that he wanted to be kept waiting for a very, very long time.

Somewhere along the way, Rox had reached the epiphany that let her know that the pain was not worth keeping close. While I sat by and nursed my wounds every chance I got. It would be a long time before my epiphany came. But I knew the second that it did, it would tear me apart before it tried to put me back together.

Then it did.

I didn't know what possessed my mother to think that a trip to *SeaWorld* was going to fix us. Fractured as my family was, we couldn't just go out in public and pretend to be happy. Hell, she had to know that I had every intention of ditching them as soon as we got into the park.

Once we were through the gate, I took off. I

didn't know where I was going or what I planned on doing, but there was no way I was going to tag around after them like the lost puppy I was. If I was going to be lost, I'd do it of my own volition and figure things out when I decided that I wanted to be found.

I made it as far as the gift shop before my world shifted. A head of brown hair appeared between the crowd and it felt like the ground beneath my feet had turned to sand. Somewhere in my life, an hourglass turned. This moment was the start of something else. Something more. And that knowledge rocked through my body with a rush that left me feeling cold and numb.

"Matt."

Not loud enough. He couldn't hear me. I forced myself to take another step, trying again.

"Matt! Matt!"

A few heads turned toward me, but not the one I wanted. It had to be him. I would know him anywhere.

I filled my lungs to try one more time, and the word died on my tongue. Turning to face me, a broad smile filled the face of my ex-boyfriend. Then he held his arms out wide.

I flew into them. One minute there was ten feet separating us and a handful of people. The next, my arms were locked like a vice around his neck, and he was squeezing me like he would never let go.

My eyes closed and I breathed in for all I was worth. He smelled like Matt. He felt like Matt. And yet, I couldn't help but wonder if this was all some twisted, sadistic dream. If Nathan was One with Cedar Creek, then Matt acted as a lighthouse, guiding me home.

As I continued to cling to him, I began to see every moment of my life that Matt had been a part of. From the first day he rode past me on his bike. When we first met at the lake. How nervous he had made me feel and how precious our relationship had been. Every second I'd spent with him flew across the backs of my eyelids, until the tears washed them all away.

"Hush now, Lex. It's alright. I've got you," he crooned, stroking my hair as my body shook. A fierce joy roared through me and I was shocked to find that it was physically painful. I'd gotten so comfortable being in pain that my body didn't know how to register any strong emotion in another way.

At last, I relinquished my hold on him. My legs felt shaky as I lowered back onto my heels, my hands braced against his shoulders. I kept my head lowered, however, as I was afraid to see what appeared in his eyes.

Matt was having none of it, and put his hand under my chin in order to force my face up. Around us, people smiled and nudged each other, thinking we were a young couple full of love and hormones. We didn't bother giving them another impression.

Taking a deep breath, I forced my gaze to meet his. My heart crumbled in my chest. The despair in his eyes lit up like a beacon, forcing me to know just how much of a failure I was. For him to be looking at me like that, the pain on my face had to be more obvious than the scars on my arm. Thank the Gods he couldn't see those.

"Don't," I whispered, shaking my head. "Don't look at me like that."

He pulled me into another tight hug, pressing his cheek to my forehead. Then he said in the most casual voice ever, "We'll save the heavy for later. You got the fast pass, right? Time to get soaked." Matt stepped back, grabbed my hand, and proceeded to drag me around the park.

"Now the trick to this is to go on all of the wet rides first. One, because you'll dry off throughout the day. Two, because the animal shows will be packed full of kids and parents most of the day until we hit about kiddy naptime. That is the magic hour, so we'll hit up the shows then. Afterward, we chill with the animals for a bit and we'll wait until sunset for the last ride. You with me?"

My laugh sounded fractured, but it was there. Then I nodded as we raced through the quick line. Of course, we could only go so far before we hit our own length of line. While it was moving faster than the other one, it still had a distance to go on its own. Matt stood me in front of him, his arms wrapped around me like we were dating. I didn't care, I felt better in his embrace.

As we waited, he blew some of my hair away from his mouth and murmured, "So what's with the hair? And the nose?" One arm left my side in order to tap the side of his nose.

I swallowed as I tried to keep my voice casual. "The stud happened in Virginia. I saw a picture and decided that I liked the look of it. So, I got it done."

Matt snorted. "Surprised you outlived your dad's wrath on that one."

I shrugged. "Well, he almost didn't notice since I took kitchen scissors and a box of black dye to my hair. If it wasn't so shiny, I think he might have overlooked it entirely."

More space appeared between us as Matt maneuvered himself so he could see my face. "You did what?"

Again, I rolled my shoulders in a shrug. "Things were changing. I was changing too," I murmured, glancing away.

He sighed. "Then...?"

"Well, my dad was even more perturbed by my lack of finding public schooling a valuable waste of my time, so we moved to Oahu."

"Wait, run that by me again?"

"I ... was skipping a lot of class. Phone calls were made. Threats flew. And eventually my dad transferred bases again. This time to Hawaii."

"You've been cutting class? Jeez, went from zero to badass in a right hurry there, didn't ya, Sparky?"

I shoved at him, grinning despite myself. "Shut up. Anyway, things happened in Hawaii. Not the least of which was the tattoo that my mom freaked over."

His voice deadpanned. "Tattoo? You? Little Lex has a tattoo?"

We moved farther up in the line and I bobbed my head. "Yep. Came across an Elder going traditional on a guy. When everyone cleared out, I didn't. It was like we recognized each other. Before I knew it, I was lying on my stomach and having ink injected into my skin."

"Show me." It wasn't a request, but I'd missed him too much to be indignant.

Since I had a bikini on, I just pulled the tank-top over my head and dragged my hair to one side. Presenting my back to him, I closed my eyes and listened to the small inhale of his surprise. Fingers brushed over the skin. Light at first, but tracing with more emphasis when he realized it was real.

"It fits you," he murmured after a minute,

letting his hand drop. I said nothing as I pulled my shirt back on.

As we stepped up to the front of the line, I almost asked him. I almost let loose one of the thousands of questions I had about home, him, and everyone I had left behind. Instead, I kept my mouth shut. He said we would save the heavy for later, so we would save it.

"So, what about the hair now?" he asked, clearing his throat. "You didn't tell me."

I kept my face impassive as I said, "When we moved here, I got my hair fixed by professionals and had it dyed black again. A few weeks later, I met someone who had a knack for adding color. She had an idea and wanted to test it out, so I let her. It turned out pretty damn cool."

"It did," he agreed with a nonchalant shrug.

"What?" I asked, a laugh in my voice.

"Nothing. Just not a personal fan of a lot of hair dye. And I liked your natural hair color. Don't look at me like I'm challenging your right to dye your hair. I'm just saying, for me, it's a personal preference."

I chuckled a little bit and let it go. We didn't talk much after that, since that's when we got on the ride. Afterward, we were too eager to get to the next one to hold up any kind of real conversation. And we continued to save the heavy for later.

Chapter Twenty Four

ASHES ON THE WIND

There was one ride at *SeaWorld* that would let Matt and I talk. For six minutes of suspended alone time, we would look out over the Pacific Ocean at sunset and let the heavy fall. Which was why I dragged my feet the whole way there. I didn't want to say goodbye yet. I was tired of saying goodbye.

Matt and I were loaded up and we began to move along the cable. Someone turned the hourglass of my life once more and all of the happiness of the afternoon drifted away. Without thinking about it, I leaned toward Matt and pressed my lips to his.

The kiss tasted bitter. Like salty tears filled with despair. It tasted like goodbye.

Matt's eyes found mine, wide with surprise. "What was that?"

Inside of me, everything was burning up. Every memory of me and him, and that cocky, arrogant, abrasive, confident young girl I used to be. That girl who smiled and laughed, rushing headlong into any challenge with a witty comeback and all of the pride her family possessed. A girl who could never be more than a memory now. Every part of her that had ever remained within me had blown away like ashes on the wind.

My voice was flat as I answered, "That was to say goodbye to the Alexandria Ryder you once knew. It's time for the heavy, Matt."

"What are you doing here?"

"Spring Break started for us, too. Mom wanted us to visit some old friends, so we're here for a week."

I snorted. "You can't bullshit a bullshitter, Matt."

He shrugged. "I didn't say that one of those old friends wasn't you or your mom. They've been keeping in touch, you know."

Devious. Cunning. Shrewd. I wasn't sure how many synonyms I could have come up with to describe my mother, but they would all amount to the same thing. She was one conniving woman when she wanted to be.

Matt's voice dropped the casual edge and he leaned closer to me. "Lex, she's afraid for you. What's going on? Talk to me."

I turned my gaze out to stare over the ocean. "Did she say what she's afraid of?"

"She thinks you might be hurting yourself."

A grim smile played with my lips. "Never underestimate my mother, Matt. It could be the last thing you do." As I said it, I let the glamour fade from my arm.

Matt choked beside me and I closed my eyes. His hand took mine in a gentle hold, as if he were afraid he'd break me. My arm was extended out and he twisted it to examine every inch of the damage I'd inflicted upon myself. I didn't realize he was crying until a drop landed in my upturned palm.

"My God, Lex. What have you done?"

I curled my hand into a fist around the teardrop, pulling my wrist out of his grasp. Then my eyes met his and I let one cold word drop into the air between us. "Survived."

All at once, fire and fury erupted in his eyes and he flashed a harsh scowl my way. "Survived? What kind of 'survival' calls for *that*?"

My chin rose and I met his gaze with my numb expression. "My kind."

"Damn you, Lex! Don't you *dare* do that. Do *not* try to justify this to me. Do you even realize what seeing those is doing to me right now? Can you imagine the look on your mother's face when she sees these? Your father's? Hell, Lex, what would Morgan think?"

"Stop," I snarled, nice and low. "She left me. She no longer has a say in anything I do. That was her choice, and these are how I'm dealing with it."

"You're *not* dealing with it! You're sitting here marking a garden in your arm, but you're not dealing with a damn thing. What the hell happened to you? The Alexandria Ryder I knew would never have done something like this."

"The Alexandria Ryder you knew is gone!"

Silence stretched between us, stitching itself

together after my screech rent it apart. Our breathing came in shallow, ragged breaths and I knew that once we were off of this ride, we'd have to get far away from each other, or else something awful would happen.

All the while, he stared at me as if he were trying to discover who I was. What I was. He stared at me as if I really was a whole different creature. And nothing like the girl he once knew.

A fact which almost broke my heart.

If I had enough heart left to break.

Before I realized it, we were back at the platform and the door was being opened for us. I leapt out of the compartment and started walking. I darted past the other people who were disembarking and headed toward the main walkway. Matt was right behind me.

There wasn't much around us, so it didn't surprise me when Matt grabbed hold of my right arm and dragged me toward a theater. When we were out of the path of foot traffic, I wrenched my arm free and turned to face him, tears rolling down my face one by one.

"Oh, Lex," he sighed, pulling me into a hug that I didn't have the will to resist. My chin rested against his shoulder and I shook in his arms as the sobs racked through my body.

All I could think was: finally. Finally, there was someone who knew me. Someone who'd witnessed what I'd gone through and knew all the things I was capable of. Now there was someone to hold me, and knew how to comfort everything broken inside of me.

"Please, Lex. Please, promise me you'll stop. Tell me that you won't hurt yourself again. I'm begging you, Lex. Please stop." I wasn't the only one crying.

The anguish in Matt's voice tore through me, opening a new gaping wound in my chest. So much pain. It sent a wave of grief to drown me, pouring salt into the wounds as it went.

For him, I wanted to stop. I wanted to tell him that I wouldn't burn anymore. That he would never have to see a fresh mark. If I promised him I would stop, I would never have to feel his pain again.

Except that his pain was but a candle flame next to my roaring bonfire. His pain was temporary and easily soothed. He didn't need the reminder that one more day was behind him, and all he had to do was make it to the next.

I shook my head.

"Please Lex!" It was his last desperate plea. I could hear it in his voice, his breathing, the clearing of his throat. And I waited for the bargaining that would soon begin.

His words lashed at me like a hailstorm in hurricane force winds. "What do you think Nathan will say when he finds out?"

For a moment, my world stopped. I couldn't move. Couldn't breathe. My eyes wouldn't even blink as I absorbed the impact of that statement. And for sixty long, painful seconds, a pressure of guilt, pain, fear, shame, and rage compressed in my chest. I was a hair-trigger away from a full-on explosion.

My voice came out in a hollow deadpan, still too stunned to comprehend his full meaning. "He will never know."

Matt stepped back enough so that I could see the hardening of his gaze. "I won't keep this from him, Lex. Nathan needs to know."

Blistering, acidic, white-hot fury burst out of me on the shriek of a banshee. What I had thought were emotions waiting to combust inside of me turned out to be magick. It shot out and slammed into Matt, throwing him back ten feet until he hit a tree. More than that, it didn't let him go.

Power whirled around me, gathering in a miniature tornado about my feet as I stalked closer to him. The air thickened around him, pinning him to the tree with his feet six inches off the ground. On the edges of my vision, I could see scarlet sparks flashing in and out of existence as the power reacted to the elements that drove me most. And high above us, I heard the distant roar of incoming thunder.

Above all others, I was made of lightning. A child of air and fire, friend to water, and destroyer of earth. Pure electric hostility that came with an announcement only after the strike had occurred.

Stopping before Matt, my eyes blazed into his own. At the same time, my voice dropped into deadly, silken tones. "You will tell him nothing."

His gaze hardened in an instant and part of me wanted to warn him not to say anything stupid. I was drunk on power, filled with a vicious rage that I was worried I couldn't control, and the desire to do great harm. I was too un-balanced to be reasoned with. And he wouldn't reason.

Matt lowered his head as far as he could in order to glare right back at me. His words were bitten at the ends as he snapped, "How are you going to stop me?"

The air around him coalesced like hard-ening cement with just a passing thought from me. As we stared each other down, I could feel it tightening around him. Constricting until his breathing became short and shallow. Until his frantic pulse became so fast that I could almost dance to the beat. My thoughts pressed in on him as if I were trying to suffocate the life out of him.

I knew that it was getting to the point of dangerous. I knew that I should stop it. Let him go. Beg his forgiveness and swear a blood oath that it would never happen again.

That part of me wasn't in control. A beast was. Intent on survival, the beast had distorted my view of the situation and had come up with some volatile conclusions. First, Nathan must never know. Second, that Matt was the only one who knew. Third, that Matt would never get the chance to tell him.

Though he barely had room to breathe, Matt managed to bark a sarcastic laugh. Then he said in a voice that had taken on a raspy edge, "That's it. Lie to me. All those times ... you said you'd never ... hurt someone. Well, Lex ... you're hurting me. You ... lied."

His words sliced like a knife, enraging the beast but also emboldening the rational side of me. I shook my head, taking an involuntary step back. At the same time, the beast tightened the magick around his chest.

A panic blossomed inside of me so fierce, I could feel nothing else. Rage vanished. Shame and guilt disappeared. Even my never-ending skin of self-loathing melted off of me. Cold terror flooded my system, and I froze.

Still, Matt managed to speak. "Stop this, Lex! You know ... you can. I know ... you want to. Please, ... just stop all of this."

Tears rolled down my face. Unrelenting sobs shot through my body and I took another step back. The tears were flowing so freely, I couldn't even see his face. I was trembling from head to toe, my teeth chattering. I didn't know what to do. I couldn't remember how to do it. I was in a frozen state of petrification, and there was nothing I could do.

The magick around him quaked a little, allowing for the first amount of movement around his shoulders. Matt took as deep a breath as he was able before his eyes narrowed in on me one more time. This time, I knew I wouldn't be able to withstand the assault.

"Lex, if you won't stop hurting yourself for your parents, or Morgan, or me, then do it for him. Do it for Nathan, Lex. Don't let him see you hurt anymore. Do it for Nathan."

I dropped to my knees.

The terror inside of me locked up every part of my body for five endless seconds. In those precious moments, it didn't occur to me to let go of the magick. Instead, the panic caused me to slice cleanly through it, severing it from the source.

At once, the magick exploded outward from where I held Matt against the tree.

We fell at the same time. One released. One ensnared.

I was welcomed into a familiar blackness. An invitation I could not deny.

Chapter Twenty Five

STILL

Tick, tock. Tick, tock. Tick, tock.

The locket around my neck sounded more like a grandfather clock as it kept time to my heartbeat. It was still there. Broken, fractured, irreplaceable. Unbelievable. Each rhythmic beat kept on as if my whole world wasn't shattered. As if I hadn't succeeded at last in bringing it all down on my head.

The reward for which was the blackness that I had held at bay for two years, now rising up in a torrential wave and dragging me into the depths of my own mind.

I did not fight it. Did not struggle. Instead, I drifted alone within the dark.

Tick, tock. Tick, tock. Tick, tock.

A haunting lullaby drifted through the air, sending a chill down my spine with its familiar melody. Somewhere in the distance, an unfamiliar voice spoke the words, not bothering to sing to the notes being played on the piano. While the melody had been a part of me since the beginning, the words I had heard only once. In a psychometric vision offered to me by a piano. Morgan's mother, Victoria, had had a light, little girl soprano voice when she sang the lullaby that was a part of her family. Now, it was also a part of mine.

"It is a part of magic, music. Something that touches the soul in ways unexplained. It can evoke heartache, loss, sorrow. Or it will grant you wings with joy, elation, and purity of sound. Do you know what it is to feel music as if it were magic? To know the power harbored in each breath and note? Do you, Lex?"

It couldn't be...

The last time I had seen Alyssa Rice, she had gone from the body of a nine-year-old girl, into the soul of a woman nearing her twenties. It was Alyssa's greatest wish to grow into a beautiful, powerful, impressive witch and woman. Her greed and impatience cost her, and her best friend had been forced to kill her before she could reach that height.

Alyssa Rice was the reason I believed in justifiable homicide.

Victoria was the reason I knew that not all suicides were as they appeared, and justice found us all in the end.

The darkness didn't lighten. No angelic light followed her as she drew near me. There was no sight or sound of her anywhere in the depths of my mind. Yet, I felt every breath she took and her energy rippled around mine, identifying it as something intimately familiar, despite the near century that had separated us.

Swallowing hard, I answered, "Music and magick glide together for you, but my powers are rooted in plants that begin in the soil and crawl toward the heavens."

"Then breathe it in, Alexandria. Then let the magic go."

I did.

Even in the darkness of my mind, I couldn't escape the searing pain that built on my left arm. A small, red spot appeared on my skin and I shrieked as the pain consumed me. All the while, my body was frozen in a state of immobility, which somehow made it worse.

When it stopped, Alyssa was gone.

It was quiet in the way the land grew still just before a storm tore across the horizon. The air deadened as lightning gathered in some far-off place, taking half of my oxygen with it. My mouth was dry and my eyes felt like they had a lead weight hanging off the lashes. Quite an odd experience given that I was still trapped within my own skull.

"That's the feeling of knowing something waits for you, but you no longer have the energy to defy it," a voice murmured. Victoria.

"It is a half-life, what one experiences after committing a crime of such a drastic nature. There is a hole left, where once humanity filled it to the brim. For those born of fire, they rage and destroy, thinking that they can burn away the emptiness inside. Instead, it grows larger, until their own ashes devour them."

"And those born of water can cradle the hole. Pour all of their emotions into it as they try to fill it once more with humanity. But it is a bottomless pit and the water runs right through you all the same," I croaked.

If I could see her, I knew she would bow her head in agreement. "Do you know what makes the hole, Alexandria?"

I'd had a good enough look into Alyssa's head to know the answer. "Ambition."

A sigh reached me, sending ripples of energy throughout the darkness. "No, not ambition. Regret marks each of us differently. When it is not a physical scar, it turns into a pit within, devouring everything that ambition feeds it and crying that it is not enough. When you are filled with regret, nothing in your life will satisfy it or soothe you."

The scars on my arm began to warm. Then one spot began to react to little flickers of heat. Flames licked at me from the inside. As always, it was a gradual build-up, but there was always a point where I could no longer hold back.

This time, my head snapped back and I screamed my pain into the void of my own mind. The burn seared into my flesh, biting deep enough to scar.

By the time it was over, I was alone.

The sound of the locket dimmed for a moment as the beeps of a heart monitor took precedence. My eyelids were too heavy to open and I could feel the morphine making its way into my veins. As if it would do any good.

My left arm felt raw near the wrist. Another ivy leaf to mark the day. Nothing new.

"We told you," my mother hissed somewhere in the room. "It happens every night. On its own." She didn't say the word 'magick' but it was layered in there.

"Our daughter is special, doctor. There are things that happen to her that no one can understand. Just, please, at midnight, could your people up her morphine?" My father's voice was husky. Almost as if he were near tears.

I must have been dreaming. A really stupid dream. It was better in the dark.

Morgan met me in the dark. Not in a visual format, of course, but her voice was there when I slipped back into the void. The first thing I heard was her clucking her tongue at me in disapproval. I almost laughed.

"Loss is a hard thing to endure. Coupled with a complete shift of your life, it is a night terror not to be escaped. Unless you have the will for it. Do you, child?"

Long-dormant pride surged through me and my chin thrust up of its own accord. My mouth opened but no words came out. We both knew the truth, and she would brook no lies.

"Not yet," I said instead, my voice sounding young and timid.

"You will need a reason, Alexandria. A goal to help you escape the pain. You will have to want something else more than you desire to remain comfortable in your hurt."

My eyes closed and shame washed through me. Not for everything I'd done, but for the fear that flooded me when she said that. Like Rox, I was comfortable with the damage that whirled around me like a twister. What I was not comfortable with was trying to focus on what came next. After living with the pain for so long, how could I live without it? Was it even possible?

As a point, I let myself feel the hurt and the wounds that pulsed with each beat of my heart. They throbbed like an organ of their own, taunting me with their presence. Even if I did manage to grasp onto something to pull me away, would the claws ever retract? Though I could drag myself into the light, I would always cast a shadow. I could make my goal the sun, and still it could not burn away every ounce of the pain or shame that coated my skin. It was a useless endeavor.

"Nothing is useless if you want it bad enough. Tell me, Alexandria, what do you want more than anything? What desire keeps you going even when all you want is to quit?"

A flash of a red brick house, a small stone cottage, and a pair of emerald eyes smashed into me. My chest constricted and it felt like my heart was being squeezed by an invisible fist. "Home. I want to go home. More than anything."

The pain that erupted on my arm dropped me to my knees. Throwing my head back, I shrieked with a primal urgency. Molten fire roared through my veins, coalescing in that one spot where the skin felt like it was splitting apart and then cauterizing itself. Part of me wished it would race to my heart and finish what the lightning had started.

The lightning was the first thing I saw in the darkness. It flashed above me, creating spider-webs across a starless sky. There were no clouds for it to light up, and no thunder announced its presence too late. Silent flashes of jagged white flew through my purgatory, and they seemed all the more dangerous for the lack of sound.

It was unsettling, having normal things around you become something *other*. In a normal setting, lightning wouldn't mean anything. Except when it was by itself. Without the thunder, the scene shifted from something normal and expected to something wrong and unpredictable. And with each flash of brilliant electricity, the silence pressed in on me.

Every second that passed, I swore one more would drive me insane. On and on, I made the same promise to myself, and the lightning continued to flash. The only rain that came with it were the tears that rolled in silence down my face.

Chapter Twenty Six

DROWNING

"I'm afraid to touch her," my mother whispered. A pang of regret shot through me as I thought of why. If I wasn't in control of my magick, and it was going on spell memory-which was what I assumed it was doing if it kept recording the days in my arm at midnight-then her touch might trigger something nasty. I didn't want her to touch me. I was tired of hurting her.

"Mel, I don't think you'll hurt her by holding her hand." Fingers released my right hand, the first I'd realized my dad had been holding it. I heard him shift out of the chair, leaving the space open for her. She never moved.

Good. I didn't know what I was doing. It was safer this way. Safe enough.

The thoughts kept repeating as I drifted once more.

Then the air disappeared and I was drowning.

"Don't struggle."

I didn't listen. Water filled my mouth, my nose, my throat. If I didn't get air soon, it would saturate my lungs, giving them less space to work with. Even in the darkness of my mind, there were some things I wasn't willing to experience. I'd already burned at the stake once and been struck by lightning. Drowning was not for me.

With one last, vicious surge, I forced the magick through me in a heat wave that would have burned the Sahara Desert. Any trace of water vanished in a second and I dropped to my knees, breathing through a raw, scratchy throat.

"You wanted to live, so you found a way."

I didn't know this woman. Her voice had never reached my ears before, though I thought I could catch the hint of a familiar mental tone. After all of the heads I'd been in, however, it was harder to identify.

"Yes," I ground out.

"You did what I could not. What I would not."

It clicked. Freyja. The only other person I knew besides Gage who had chosen to take her own life, regardless of the consequences. Unlike Morgan or Victoria, she had no solid reasoning that said her life was meant to end. She wasn't ill and she wasn't condemned to death for committing murder. Instead, she had looked at the life she could have had, and the one she did, and she had decided that should-haves and could-haves were more important to her than what existed.

I wanted to be angry with her. It should have been easy. She was just like Gage: selfish and afraid of the future. She'd succumbed to her own blackness long before she'd ended her life.

Of course, the one reason I couldn't hate her was because we were too similar. Both of us were born with an immense amount of power, and not an inkling of what we could or should do with it.

Like me, Freyja had lived through many lives. She'd been privy to different eras where magic wasn't spelled with a k. Where witches were numerous and revered. Wizards could put kings on their thrones, even if they were barely old enough to hold a sword. And those who could access the power of the world were known for power and prestige.

They were also expected to use it with great wisdom and regard for consequences.

Twitching the weather for one afternoon was one thing. Yet, nature would get her recourse in the end. A day of sunshine could become a drought in a month. While a summer shower might deliver a monsoon. Without wisdom or appreciation, magick would do as it willed and the consequences were on the wielder.

Freyja, at some point, had been important. A leader of people. Someone revered and who was now forgotten.

I knew how she felt because I felt the same. If I looked far enough into my own past, I would find decades of life spread before me. Lives with the same power. The same reverence. Equal leadership. We were two sides to a coin.

Except, life had squeezed all of the ambition out of her and had left her with a gaping hole of regret. In the world we had entered now, the old ways were bathed with new rules. Societies ran on different ideals. Respect and honor were things with fickle definitions, and the whole world was booking itself a one-way ticket to Hell in a handbasket.

It was not a good world for a Sensitive to live in. Too much pain and disgrace was apparent. In the end, there were only two choices available to women like us: deal with it, or leave everyone else to their own devices.

I dealt with it.

Freyja abandoned ship.

"Are you really dealing? Or are you abandoning it all in another way?"

That hit a little too close to home.

"Do you know what it is to drown, sister? To feel every muscle in your body rebel against an element of nature, until you could fight it no longer. It is not as you see it in the movies. There is no thrashing or screaming. Only the gulps of air as you try to push the water back to the depths.

"In the end, however, the fatigue overwhelms you. As you sink below the surface, it is not peaceful. It is painful. Your lungs burn with the fury of the sun until the very last second. Then, it all begins to fade, until there is nothing left.

"This is your drowning, sister. You are amidst your own depths and are taking gasps of air that are coming fewer and farther between. Soon, you must decide as you just did. You must gather your final reserves and push to the surface. Or you will join me in the depths, and we will know again that we were not strong enough for this world.

"Will you admit that defeat?"

No. I would not.

I was not like her. I was a survivor. Come what may. Hell could throw whatever demon dogs it had at me, because I wasn't going down without a fight.

And I'd be damned if some stupid part of my brain tried to finish the job.

This time, I barely felt the burn as it worked into my skin. Instead, I focused on the heated determination sweeping through me.

There was a way out of this, but it would take me time to find it.

I was almost ready to try.

"Sometimes I wonder if you would even recognize your soulmate if he or she was standing in front of you. Would you, Alex?"

For a minute, I couldn't think of the answer, since I was too busy wondering what Rox's voice was doing in my head. I was getting used to the dead-people-only conversations, so this one freaked me out a little. If she had gone through with her 'meet Gage in the afterlife' plan, I would exorcise her ass.

"I'm not dead. I'm just ... present."

That did not explain nearly enough, but it was a good thing to know in any case.

"Alex, focus."

Taking a deep breath, I thought back to her original question. Then a smile pulled at my lips. "I'm not like you, Rox. I don't believe that we all have only one soulmate. There are more than enough people in this world that will fit together with you like a puzzle piece. It's just rather difficult for most people to find them."

"It wasn't difficult for you."

I shook my head. "No. It wasn't."

Faces flashed before me and my smile grew

sad. I saw my parents. Morgan. Nathan and Matt. Even Nathan's mother, Anne Richards.

"You can be a soulmate without having a romantic interest," I informed her. "A soulmate just means that you belong with each other in this world, in some capacity. Maybe as parents, lovers, or friends. I've found most of mine. How many have you found, Rox?"

She didn't answer. I didn't expect her to.

Heat built in my arm and I gritted my teeth as I braced for the pain. As I was burning, one more soft question pierced through the dark.

"Would you know he was your soulmate if you were staring right at him?"

Chapter Twenty Seven

FICKLE

I expected Gage next. If not him, George or Benjamin could show up. If we were dragging every ghost of my life through my mind, those were the only ones left that could offer insight into my own fractured heart.

Matt could also appear, if we were going to grab random living people and throw them into the dark, too. Though I doubted Matt would be able. He didn't know the dark like Rox and I did. Which was good. I never wanted him to know what it was like.

Of course, there was one person that knew the dark as well as I did, but I wasn't ready to see him. For him to appear, I would know with absolute certainty just how low a person I was. How far I had dragged him down, and what it cost him to be my friend. My anchor.

Nathan was the most stable thing in my life, and I was the most erratic thing in his. If he stumbled into the dark, I knew it would be because of me. And I would hate myself forever for being able to do that to him.

"Why do you take the blame for everything?" Gage sighed somewhere in the blackness. "What makes you think everything revolves around you?"

I almost snorted. "During your life, did everything not revolve around you? If I weren't at the center of everything, maybe I wouldn't think that."

"Just because you're in the center doesn't mean you're the reason everyone else's life turned out the way it has. Just means you were a part of their lives. Not that every decision involved you."

"Doesn't mean I didn't have a hand in the biggest decisions. Or trigger the most important consequences."

"Importance is relative. Do you think, at the end of your life, you'll look back at that day in SeaWorld and call it the most important moment of your life? After everything life will hand you, you can't decide which was the most important until the end. And you might be surprised which memory you choose when it comes down to it."

He was wrong. The moment the words settled around me, I knew that it wouldn't take a lifetime to decide which moment of my life was the most important. It was as clear to me as ever, standing at the gate, staring up at a red brick house coated in ivy when I was nine years old. Of everything that happened to me in my life, I knew that it was in that moment that everything had begun. Morgan, Nathan, magick, everything was an extension off of that one single moment in time. No matter what came next, it would all trace back to that house in New England.

Fire licked along my arm, curling up by my wrist and burrowing deep into my skin. My teeth dug into my bottom lip as it gained in intensity. This time, I didn't scream.

Love is a fickle creature, absorbed in its own ideals and romanticisms. It is a combination of reality and fantasy, and decides on its own how much balance is required before it will flourish. Otherwise, it will wither, leaving those once touched by it destitute and downtrodden. Too much reality and the fantasy will buckle. So many fictions cannot obscure a truth without consequence. A great amount of work went into keeping a love strong and alive.

It took no effort at all for a love to bloom.

All it took was a moment. A single glance amidst a celebration. Our gazes latched onto one another at a distance, before the movements of the dance tore my eyes from his. My heart felt full of joy and I released the laughter alongside my friend and her sister as we were spun about by the other maidens of the village. Spring was in full bloom, and this wedding marked the first of many for the season.

Whenever the opportunity was afforded to me, I sought out the man talking with the bride and groom. His eyes searched for mine almost in the same instant. It was enough to cause my cheeks to blaze and my soul to writhe with pleasure. With each moment, I became even more certain that I was looking into my future, and this man was standing there.

It was almost a trial to wait until the dance had ended. My impatience had grown when I noticed Sarah Ellis approach and be introduced to him. Though she had spent little time in speaking with him—Elizabeth and Sarah being known to disapprove of one another—I knew the kind of impression a woman of her beauty could make upon a man. Though I harbored her no ill will, it would be more than daunting should his attention turn to her instead of me.

When we had stopped spinning at last, I took a moment to be sure I would not stumble. Satisfied, I approached Elizabeth with all of the impertinence allowed to her best friend. Upon her wedding day, it would be unusual for me not to stand beside her at times. Thus was my reasoning when I interrupted the gathering.

My friend was not at all fooled by my demeanor, and reached out a hand for mine as soon as she noticed my approach. "Mary! Mr. Sullivan, you must allow me to introduce you to my dearest companion, Mary Smith. Mary, this is Mr. William Sullivan."

It took my best effort not to scoff at her lack of subtlety. As it was, my attention was arrested by the most handsome man I had ever seen. William Sullivan was a tall enough man, with a lean but powerful build. His skin was tanned, with cobalt eyes appearing more striking for the contrast. Dark brown hair was tied back at the nape of his neck, but for a slight curl that would fall over his forehead as though it could not remember its place.

For so long had we stood looking at one another, I did not realize when another had stolen my friend's company. Even more time elapsed before either of us spoke a word. At last, when I heard his voice for the first time, I was almost shocked by the gentle question it held.

"Would you care to dance?"

I placed my hand in his, not daring to tear my gaze from his. In my heart grew the steady knowledge that I could glimpse my whole world in those clear blue eyes.

I blinked once and the blue eyes were replaced with emerald. The people around us vanished, and we were standing on a familiar road with a gate to my left. Nathan reached for me and I stepped into the embrace.

It was like gasping in that first, rich breath of oxygen after a long submersion. Air to drowning lungs. And as I clung to him, the inside of my wrist began to prickle with the heat.

I didn't let go. Even when the pain became unbearable. Even when I pressed my mouth to his shoulder and screeched into his t-shirt. Even when the tears fell onto the fabric, soaking it as the fire continued to rage over the veins and tendons just below my palm.

I clung to the illusion that was Nathan until the fire died. Then he was gone and I had an empty, sideways hourglass to mark the day that I had left him.

Two years to the day.

Chapter Twenty Eight

FREE

Before the hourglass, I'd lost all track of time. Didn't bother to count the scars. Had no need to keep track of how often I slipped into some level of consciousness.

After the hourglass, I began to keep track of the days. There was but one day that would mark itself in such a way and would let me cling to a phantom of my best friend. The day I said goodbye to him.

From there, it was easy to track the days by each scar that appeared. Though it was so black that I couldn't see my own hand in front of my face, I could feel every burn that bit into my flesh and I knew that my arm was reaching its limit. Part of me also knew that, when it did, I would finally be done with it all.

It was also something that limited the conversations that I'd been having. My being aware was important. When I drifted too far, they came and spoke to me. Yet, when I was aware and waiting, that was when they vanished.

In between tracking days and waiting for conversations from the dark, I was able to ponder the memory. It was mine, I knew. More mine than anyone else's, at any rate.

Mary Smith had been the birth name of the woman who had burned at the stake in Cedar Creek. It was her murder by the hands of her own coven that had caused the balance to shift in the circle, leaving an oily feeling over the shield that protected it. A burning I had felt every horrific moment of during my Wiccaning when I was nine. Now I knew why my Wiccaning-a strong blessing-offset the evil of her burning. She was my past life.

When I was in the head of someone else, I could always think my own thoughts. Remark on my surroundings in my own voice, while getting an inside look into their thought processes. With Mary, I got none of that. I lived it. Which meant I had lived it.

That wasn't a vision. It was a memory so old and so potent that I hadn't been able to disengage from it. Just like my burning.

The lightning was back. This time, thunder rolled with it across my world. A small comfort, considering the day. Somewhere in the dark, my mind was conjuring a great storm filled with a whipping wind, stinging rain, and roiling clouds.

None of it was real. I knew that, but I couldn't make myself give it all up just yet. Turning in place, I glided through the dark, trying to find the circle that brought me purpose and ripped my world apart in the same instant. That was the balance.

I didn't expect voices of the night while the lightning raged. What I got instead sent goosebumps all down my arms. The lullaby was back, though no one sang the words this time.

When I woke up in Morgan's bed hours after I had been burned at the stake, I'd heard the same strange song. It had called to me, promising magick and power in its lilting melody. That hadn't changed.

I had.

As the lightning flared above me and thunder rolled in a long, deep voice, I continued to glide beneath the clouds that my mind had conjured. The lullaby merged with the wind, until there was less howling and more music. And when the storm unleashed the icy rain, it sounded like tribal drums battering the ground.

While the rain pounded over me, I thought of my dad and how we used to run outside to dance. I would throw my head back and laugh as he spun me around. We wouldn't stop until we both fell. That was the deal: both down and done. If one of us remained upright at any time, we still had a date.

Taking a deep breath, I let the thought go. Another rose in its place. Matt and I racing along the trail from the lake. Both of us laughing as the rain fell down around us. Then that single moment that he decided was perfect. I could still feel the taste of my first kiss on my lips. And as a gate separated us, Matt had beckoned me to him one more time to steal another before he headed home.

The happy memories faded, replaced by one that tore my heart in two. It was this memory that the storm came for.

Once more, I was in the circle. Standing at the center, my eyes rose to the sky. I watched as the lightning gathered into a bright, piercing ball of light. A moment later, it exploded, arching down and slamming into my chest.

Even here, I felt myself fall onto my back, pinned into place by the strike. And as I was lying there in the blackness of my mind, another heated blast erupted on my arm. My back arched as the oleander blossomed on my inner forearm.

When the pain subsided, I knew which day it was. The day Morgan had committed suicide and my world had dived into a spectacular tail-spin.

For several long minutes, I stayed on the ground and panted as the last of the storm vanished. It was as if it had never existed.

Awareness hammered into me, causing my heart to jump. I stumbled to my feet, twisting about in the dark. I waited. With bated breath and a heart beating so hard that it hurt, I waited.

"Lex." Somewhere in the dark, it was a shout. When it reached me, it was but a whisper.

My entire body rocked with a hard shiver. Trusting my instincts, I twisted in the dark and took off at a steady jog. Once more, I heard my name being called in the distance. I was getting closer.

He kept calling my name. I refused to answer. Instead, I continued running until the whispers became spoken word. Until they grew to a raised voice. Tears stung my eyes when I heard them as a shout. When I could hear him yelling with the full force of his voice, I began to sprint.

His name tore from my throat on a sob the second I glimpsed him in the dark. "Nathan! Nathan! *Nathan!*"

I almost couldn't see his face through the tears, but I would know that smile anywhere. In the same instant, he headed toward me. His long legs ate away at the distance and I pushed myself even faster.

This time, there was no fear. There would be no wall rushing down on us. Nothing could separate us now. At long last, I would be in his arms and I would remember what home felt like.

Nathan and I crashed into each other, our momentum spinning us around as we tried not to fall. When we regained our footing, I threw myself into his arms at the same time he pulled me to him. We clung to each other with the single-mindedness of two people who had been kept waiting for too long.

Minutes that felt like seconds passed before I felt his arms loosen. My vice grip around his neck relaxed a little, and Nathan moved his head back far enough so I could see into those deep emerald eyes. In them, I saw a longing so intense that it was depthless.

When he spoke, it was as if he were casting a spell of his own. With Nathan's one request, I was set free.

"Come home, Lex. Come home."

Tick, tock. Tick, tock. Tick, tock.
Thump-thump. Thump-thump. Thump-thump.

Chapter Twenty Nine

PEACE

This time I recognized the heart monitor for what it was: not a dream. In slow motion, I became aware of the reality surrounding me. Drips of some fluid entering an IV tube sticking out of my right arm. Heavy boots paced from one side of the room to the other. Someone shifted in a vinyl-covered chair in the corner.

And right inside of my left elbow, where all of my veins gathered to supply my arm with my heart's blood, the heat began to recede. With the speed of a zombie, I cracked my eyelids open and glanced at the spot. A valerian flower was still bathed in the red of injured flesh, marking it as my drug of choice.

It hadn't hurt.

"Damn it, where's that nurse?" my dad snarled. "They know what happens at midnight."

"John," my mother sighed. My eyes darted to her, blinking to clear some of the crud holding them closed. Her eyes flew wide and an almost soundless plea fell from her lips. "John."

"I can't do this. God, I cannot do this," he ground out as he turned by the door and started pacing back to my mother.

Without taking her eyes from mine, she reached out a hand and tried in vain to catch his attention. "John. John!" Her voice had grown frantic and my dad finally glanced up at her.

It took him a second to understand. As soon as he saw where she was looking, his eyes snapped to me. I was slow to meet his gaze, but when I did, I tried to offer up a tiny smile.

I almost stopped breathing, I was hit with such a massive amount of love from both of them. Love and gratitude. Joy and relief. It washed over me like sunlight, warming every part of my body with a blissful heat.

What I had told Rox had been true. Soulmates took on many forms. What mattered was that they were with you, no matter the cost. For my parents, that cost had been high. Too high. And that was my doing. A betrayal I would work the rest of my life to rectify.

Starting with a penance.

A long time ago, Nathan's mother, Anne, had told me that magick and mundane had to be given an equal balance in one's life, or there would be consequences. At the time, I was a thirteen-year-old pain in the ass, and I'd discounted her wisdom. After three years, it had finally bitten me, too.

Given that I had lived with nothing but a constant stream of magick for two years straight, it was time to pay it back. I would let the valerian in my arm be the last of it to leave me. No matter the consequences.

My smile grew wider as I studied my parents. Then I held up my right hand and reached for my mother. "Don't be afraid, Mommy. Please?"

I'd been in a coma for five months. I went under when the magick hit me on April sixth, and didn't wake up until August's Friday the Thirteenth. One blink of my life, and I lost five whole months. Pieces of my life that I could never get back.

Somehow, I was okay with that. In some twisted way, those five months meant more to me than the two years that preceded them.

After two years of lashing out, making dramatic changes, and antagonizing my parents into a pit of despair, I had accomplished nothing. I had hurt no one in the ways that I was hurting. The pain could not be stopped. Nor had I even considered healing. For two years, I was nothing short of an absolute wreck.

Within five months, I had learned to deal with everything I had tried to avoid. Most of all, I learned to deal with the loss. That was the hardest part. Saying goodbye all over again was like rubbing a salted lemon into a stab wound. What was left afterward, however, was priceless.

Peace.

I made peace with the fact that I couldn't help Morgan.

I made peace with the people of Cedar Creek who'd had me on trial for murder.

I made peace with my parents for wanting to protect me and taking me away.

I made peace with myself for not being able to stay.

I made peace with myself for the suffering I put my parents through.

I made peace with myself for what I had done to Matt.

I made peace with myself for the five months I had lost.

I even made peace with what I had put Nathan through. Mostly because I intended to pay back that debt for the rest of my unnatural life.

He would never see it in the light that I did, but somewhere inside, we both knew that he saved my life. There were but two ways to handle the dark: seek out the light, or succumb to the blackness. I could have wandered that darkness for years, or I could have succumbed to it in another month or two. Without Nathan to act as my light, anything was possible. But he had.

Nathan was the best friend I would ever have. A soulmate of a different sort, I knew our bond could only be reinforced by this experience. Though it was built on four years of silence, a year of laughter, and two more years of shared nightmares, I knew that the moment we crashed into one another in the dark, we were bound by something stronger than steel cables.

When I returned to Cedar Creek, I would be returning to Nathan, too. In the meantime, I was going to try my damnedest to make the years between as guiltless as possible. I was tired of feeling ashamed.

I hefted the box of books up onto my hip, grunting at the effort. It lasted about two seconds before my mom darted over and lifted the box out of my hand in a maneuver that left me with one hip still cocked to the side.

"Hey!"

"Hey, nothing. You ran on fluids for five months. When you put a little more meat on your bones, then you can start carting around thirty-pound boxes of books. Until then, you can handle some of the lighter stuff."

I scowled after her as she marched out the front door toward the moving truck. My dad added insult to injury by pressing a box marked 'pillows' into my hands. The smirk on his face as he kept walking almost erased my irritation. Almost. Shaking my head, I picked up another light box and followed my parents out to where the truck waited.

It was still surreal, knowing that this was all happening. My Gunnery Sergeant father had officially retired. No more bases. No more orders or commands for him. He'd gotten out. For me.

He'd never admit that, of course. Not that I ever asked him. Didn't need to. Five months changed everything, and I really was the center of the universe-no matter what Gage said.

After I passed off my boxes to my mother-who was moving around in the back of the truck, determined to organize it into perfect unpacking scenarios-I stepped back and found a familiar blonde standing across the street.

Rox and I locked eyes for a second before her gaze dropped to the ground. A fist squeezed my heart and I didn't bother to look both ways as I went to meet her. I had to give her credit, she didn't run.

"So, it's true," she muttered. "You're really leaving."

I nodded. "Couldn't stay forever."

Her eyes raised to mine. "I was hoping."

A knife inserted itself into my lung, making it hard to breathe. "I'm sorry, Rox. I wasn't the friend to you that you deserved."

She tried to smile. "You were the friend I needed. That means more than anything else I could have asked for."

My smile was easier to come by. "Thank you. I'm glad to have met you, Rox." With her permission, I pulled her into a hug.

"Me too, Alex."

We didn't say that we'd miss each other. We wouldn't. Nor did we exchange information. Neither of us would use it. It was a simple goodbye, if such things ever could be. Some people were meant to stay in someone's life for but a short time. Rox and I were one of those for each other. And after I left, we would be memories placed in a box labeled with the darkest days of our lives. It was the best place for us.

When Rox had gone, I headed back into the house. The minute my foot crossed the threshold, the phone began to ring. Some presentiment ran through me as I moved into the kitchen. I didn't bother to look at the Caller ID before I picked up the phone. No need.

The first words Matt said to me were, "Don't apologize."

ACKNOWLEDGEMENTS

We're at the hard part again. Trying to piece together all of the loose strands of book publishing and thanking everyone who was involved. Even snatching at pieces of my real life and the people who make sure I eat and drink during one of my writing bouts. Without further ado, let us dive in.

My best friend, Chrissy, deserves all of the praise for this book reaching anyone's hands. Cover designer, interior formatter, occasional editor, and all-around ass-kicker. She is also the most compassionate, sensitive, endearing, and engaging person I know. I love everything about you, but especially the way your mind and heart work. You're special in every way a human could be, and I love being a part of your life and having you in mine.

I would also like to thank my editing team: Connie and Liz. Though life was hectic, they pulled through for me. They questioned, poked, prodded, and eliminated many of the errors I was bound to make. For which, I am immeasurably grateful. You both also make some of the best friends a person could have. I'm so happy to have your support even this many years later.

For all of their love and support, I must thank my Nana and Papa. Without them, I never would have discovered my joy or ambition for this career of mine. Thank you both for keeping me afloat all of the times I was drowning. Even when you didn't know my head was underwater.

My Big Dude always comes next. For her patience and ability to let me be me. She is a constant supporter of my dreams, and I would not have a life without her. You are the reason I'm still here; that's how much I love you.

Christopher is a bigger part of my story than he will ever know. He's one of four reasons that I have a story left at all. He's one of the few reasons I keep going with the stories that I still have in me. Thank you, honey, for all of the adventures. I love you.

Lastly, I have to thank my friends. While I would prefer to do that in alphabetical order and list every name, I don't think we have room or time for that. Rest assured, you know who you are. And you know why I'm saying this next:

We can't help others until we help ourselves. Unless we decide to do so, no one else will be capable of it.

You guys didn't save me. But you made it so that I wanted to save myself. Every time I started to slip into the dark, you guys gave me a reason to see the light. Thank you so much for that.

To everyone I haven't named, as well as everyone already mentioned, you have no idea how your presence has changed my life. I am grateful for that every single day.

ABOUT THE AUTHOR

Hollow Ryan is a Michigan native with thirty years spent too much in her own head, and twenty years putting it all on paper. This obsession with the written word has led her to publish the five-book paranormal series, *The Prideful Magick Collection*. It has also started her on a journey full of *Demon Kin*.

When not working on her ever-expanding Work List, Hollow is dealing with the three most spoiled fur-children to be found in Northeastern Michigan. (Her spouse is absolutely to blame for that.)

For more information, please visit:
www.hollowryan.com

Hawthorn

PRIDEFUL MAGICK COLLECTION
BOOK FOUR

Chapter One

FIRST IMPRESSIONS

Fixing things and starting over had become second nature. Even so, I wasn't sure I'd learned enough to fix this.

"This is why I wasn't allowed to see him before closing," I remarked, my nose wrinkling at the ugly green house.

My mom grinned at me in that way that declared she was entirely unrepentant about her decision. I almost couldn't keep a straight face, knowing she was where I got that from.

"He'll take us all year and drain all of our reserves, you know."

"We know," she answered, unperturbed. "But he'll be grand when he's finished."

I fought the smile as best I could, shaking my

head at her optimism. Releasing a sigh, I said, "The first thing I'm going to need is a privacy fence for that backyard."

"You can see it already, can't you?"

Looking back at the house, my eyes grazed over the 'before' image and were rewarded with an 'after' a second later. Nodding to my mom, I said, "Yeah, I can see it."

"Then you know it'll all work out."

"It always does."

It was our new family motto. An exchange that rose from the ashes of my sixteenth year and the five months I spent in a coma. Whenever things seemed difficult or we stretched ourselves too thin, all three of us thought back to our darkest days and knew that we could overcome anything after having lived through them.

"Want to see the inside?" Mom asked, breaking into my reverie.

"Do I have to?"

"Unless you want to spend the night on the curb."

My eyes lowered to the sidewalk before shooting back to the house. Twisting my features into a considering expression, I pretended to debate my choices. Mom chuckled before grabbing hold of my wrist to pull me up the walk. As soon as she realized what she was doing, she dropped my hand like she'd been burned. Again.

Hurt shot through me and I worked to keep it off of my face. Her reaction was to be expected. A mere two years ago, I'd made sure the threat held. It would take her more time than that to fall back into old habits.

Not that we would ever get back to what we were. The time of my perfect and easy relationship with my parents was long gone. Buried beneath a sea of bodies, omissions, and betrayals. It was impossible for the three of us to reconcile the old wounds. But we could move past them.

Forcing a smile and chipper tone, I linked my arm through my mother's and gestured toward the crumbling heap before us. "Come on, Mom. Show me the rest of this palace that you and Dad stole."

The itch to transform the drab clay color into a burnt orange was almost overwhelming as I stared at the four walls of my attic bedroom. It didn't help that I could see clearly the growing brown spot that indicated where the roof had been leaking. If I used just a little bit of magick-

I shut the thought off right then and there. No more magick. At least for a while. When I could put the mundane back in balance with the magick, then I could reopen that door. Until then, it was normal living for me.

At least it was getting easier. When I'd first cut off my magick, it had been almost impossible to ignore the pulsing inside of me that begged to be used. After a year, however, the barest flutter drifted over my skin as the magick acknowledged my desire, but respected my restraint.

With a sigh, I turned to my desk and added 'check for mold' to my to-do list. Then I plugged in the alarm clock and set the time on it before climbing into bed. One more first night in a new house. Then would come my first day in a new town. Following that was my first day in a new school. After experiencing the same set of firsts several times before this, I was no longer emotional about them.

Except this time. Because this time was the last set of firsts I would have. This would be the last time I lived under my parents' roof. The last new thing we shared. After this, I was going back to everything that was familiar and haunting.

For the first time, the rest of my life didn't seem so far away.

My expectations for Grant didn't exist. As with my past schools, I never felt the need to integrate into the small societies I passed through. Being in a town for only a few months at a time, it meant I was able to go unnoticed. I enjoyed every scrap of anonymity that was available to me. Especially since I knew it would not last much longer.

The first day of school brought with it the usual excitement, and I was engulfed in that chaos as soon as I walked through the door. At the same time, it was as if the building radiated a certain expectation, and even though I'd gone mundane, I could have sworn there was magick embedded in its bricks.

I was still in a kind of confused daze while consulting the papers sent to my house after I was registered. One page contained my schedule, another a map, and a third my locker information. None of which proved to be much help.

When I felt the girl approaching, I had no idea she meant to actually engage with me until she said, "No offense, but you look like a lost puppy. Let me help you."

Looking up at her, I was surprised by how pretty her brown eyes were. "Um..."

"Can I see?" she asked, ignoring my discomfort. Knowing it couldn't hurt, I passed her the paper with my locker information on it. She raised her eyes to mine again and smiled. "Mine's not too far off. I'll show you."

She didn't even wait for a response, instead turning and melting into the crowd. I had no choice but to roll my eyes and follow after her. Thankfully, we didn't have far to go from the front door as she led me down a few hallways. We entered a corridor with a wall of windows on the left, looking out at the courtyard, with lockers covering the wall on the right. At once, the girl stopped and spun around to face me, sending her skirt flaring out around her.

"Here we are," she announced with a wide smile.

"Thanks..."

"Oh, yeah, name, right," she laughed. "I'm Delaire, but you can call me Del."

I grinned. "Alexandria. I prefer Alex." For strangers, at least.

"It's nice to meet you, Alex. And sorry about the 'lost puppy' comment. You just…"

"Looked like a lost puppy. I got it," I said with a grin. "It's okay. I'm kind of used to it at this point."

One eyebrow rose and I had to admire how artful her expression was. "Move around a lot?" she asked, leaning against the lockers as I entered the combination on mine.

"You could say that. Three houses in the past year, not counting my dad's military moves prior to then."

"Oh? That sounds intriguing."

More than she knew, though I wasn't about to tell her that. Instead, I emptied my bag of the binders I'd set up for my classes and stacked them on the too-small shelf at the top of the locker. Then I shrugged out of my jacket and hung it up inside.

When I returned my attention to Delaire, her teak eyes were running up my body in silent contemplation. The moment she realized I'd noticed, she grinned and said, "You don't care much for first impressions, do you?"

I shrugged. "They don't matter much if you don't intend to impress anyone."

She bowed her head in acknowledgement. "Fair enough. I still find myself doing the whole dress-up bit for my first day, though. Makes me feel powerful and alluring." I laughed as she ended the description with a dramatic pose.

"I think I'm going more for the 'forgettable and unnoticed' vibe."

An eyebrow arched upward. "I don't think that's going to work."

Before I could ask, the doors at the end of the corridor burst open. A magick breeze pushed through the corridor, almost physically moving students out of the way. I raised my eyebrows at the dramatic display before my eyes narrowed in on four women standing on the other side of the threshold.

They strode into the school, each abreast of another. The first was a statuesque beauty with flashing green eyes and long, brown hair. Beside her was a golden blonde whose expression radiated a haughty disdain for others. A redhead followed them, though there was enough brown in her hair to warrant the label of 'auburn.' At last, however, entered a true marvel. White hair and icy blue eyes were the defining markers of the youngest girl, which somehow seemed to negate the fact that she was almost as pretty as the three that came before.

If it were only that they were beautiful and dramatic, I might not have taken notice of them. But that wasn't all. With each step that they took, a pulse of magick reached me. Fresh and thriving from the eldest. Scorching and intense. Contemplative and aloof. Cold and isolated. Together, they were a force to be reckoned with, and I had to believe it was a rare thing for them to be separated.

"We call them the Season Sisters."

As if Delaire's words were a trigger, their eyes latched onto me. At once, their magick surged forward, seeking what they knew I kept buried. Something that was eager to respond.

I could feel it pulsing inside of me. A beacon that was bursting through my ribcage with each rapid beat of my heart. The magick fluttered through my veins, awakening every cell of my body as it tried to combat the intrusion. Their intent was to identify other witches, and my magick was eager to exploit just how useful a vessel I was.

As casually as I could manage, I raised my hand to the locket around my neck. Habit forced the magick out of me and poured it into the gears that caused the little clock to keep time. It was something I'd done so often in the past year that I almost couldn't feel what Morgan or her eldest daughter, Freyja, had added to it in the past.

Their magick spiked with the depletion of mine and their curiosity permeated the hallway. Four sets of eyes were locked on me as they each seemed to debate whether or not introducing themselves was something they wished to endure. In the end, the eldest sister squared her shoulders and turned away.

Another pulse of magick shot out from the second girl and I caught my breath as my magick once more leapt to the surface. This time, I let it linger. Just long enough to help me take stock of my surroundings. My mouth fell open.

"There are over thirty witches in this school,"

I murmured. Then I let my eyes meet Delaire's. "Why so many?"

She gave me an almost weary smile as she announced, "Because you are in the heart of Crone's Crescent territory. And you just met their princess."